ONE STEP FROM HELL

•

John M. Sharpe

AVALON BOOKS
NEW YORK

Published by Avalon Books, an imprint of
Thomas Bouregy & Co., Inc.
160 Madison Avenue, New York, NY 10016

Library of Congress Cataloging-in-Publication Data

Sharpe, John M.
 One step from hell / John M. Sharpe.
  p. cm.
 ISBN 978-0-8034-7791-9
 I. Title.
 PS3619.H3566O54 2010
 813'.6—dc22
                        2010016289

PRINTED IN THE UNITED STATES OF AMERICA
ON ACID-FREE PAPER
BY HADDON CRAFTSMEN, BLOOMSBURG, PENNSYLVANIA

Chapter One

Royce leaned an elbow against a bar that was scarred with countless cigar burns and even a few bullet holes, and he gazed with little real interest around the smoky cantina.

Along the bar, two young vaqueros, broad sombreros thrown back from their heads and six-shooters on their hips, were urging drinks on a middle-aged woman who looked as though she had already had a few too many. In one corner, an old man sat strumming tunelessly on a battered guitar, while four other men sat at a table drinking, smoking, and playing some kind of a dice game that Royce had never seen before. They looked serious and didn't seem to be enjoying the game very much.

Royce took a gold-plated watch out of his shirt pocket and checked the time. He was bored. There was nothing to do in this grubby little Mexican town. So far he hadn't been able to find the man he had come to kill, and he needed some excitement. Anything, any action would do. That's why he had put a big bet on the cockfight that

1

was going on out in the street. But the bird he had bet on probably wouldn't be fighting for another twenty minutes or so, and Royce was growing restless. He looked at his watch again.

He was about to ask the dark, fat little bartender for another glass of tequila when he was stopped by the sounds of shouting and hooting and whistling from outside. Royce went quickly to the open door and stood watching as the circle of men in the middle of the dusty square parted. A sad-faced man, carrying a bloody, lifeless game bird, pushed through the crowd, ambled away, and was quickly lost among the people lounging in front of the small shops and open-air markets that lined the street.

A somber Mexican paid off the smiling winners, and some of them drifted away while the others from the broken circle milled around listlessly and a few curious, barefoot children joined the crowd. Obviously the fight had ended sooner than anyone had expected. That meant Royce's bird was due to fight now. He felt a slight twinge of excitement as he imagined the pending violence. Royce liked violence, thrived on it. Then he saw the old man approach the center of the still loosely formed group. He was smiling and gently stroking the head of the brightly plumed bird he held under one arm. It was the bird Royce had bet on so heavily.

A young man dressed in a straw sombrero and the white cotton clothes of a typical *peón,* with dusty sandals on his bare feet, appeared from a side street. He held a drab-colored gamecock in both hands, its head concealed under a leather hood. The human circle began to re-form, and the young man moved to its center where the old man waited. He slipped the hood off his bird's head and, still holding it with both hands, thrust it, beak forward, toward the old man, who thrust his rooster out in the same way. With feathers ruffled, the birds pecked at each other viciously while a buzz of excitement went up from the human arena as it pressed closer.

Royce moved from the doorway to the edge of the circle and found a spot where he could watch the action. He smiled, feeling a shiver of anticipation similar to what he'd felt before each of the countless showdowns he had faced in his violent career.

In the ring, the birds circled each other warily, their neck feathers ruffled as they pecked at each other tentatively, as if instinctively seeking an advantage. Then, in a flurry of dust and feathers, and amid yells from the crowd, the old man's bird launched a furious attack, his flapping wings carrying him to just the right height to enable him to strike with his razor-sharp spurs. The crowd noise swelled, and Royce smiled at the display of innate cruelty, and at the thought of the easy money that would soon be his. But the young man's bird retaliated swiftly. With his neck feathers fully extended, his beak slashed at the other bird's head, drawing blood and dislodging a cascade of feathers. Then the young man's bird was hovering in the air, its furiously flapping wings raising a cloud of dust while its lethal spurs hacked and sliced at its opponent's head and neck. And suddenly the fight was over. The crowd stood in stunned silence while the winning bird strutted around the circle pausing only to issue a loud crow of victory and to scratch dust on the limp body of his victim.

Royce was stunned. He felt cheated—not just because of the money he had lost, but also because he had been deprived of the lengthy violent spectacle that he had expected. Now, as the crowd drifted away mumbling in disbelief, he sought out the old man. He found him kneeling in the dust holding his lifeless bird in his hands, his face filled with grief and anguish. Royce walked over to him and stood, spread legged, glaring down at him.

"You owe me fifty pesos, amigo."

The old man glanced up, a questioning look in his mournful eyes. "*¿Qué? No comprendo, señor.*"

Royce drew his .45 and aimed it at the old man's head. "You *comprendo* this?" The few remaining onlookers shrank back, and wide-eyed children stared in fascination. Somewhere a woman screamed. Royce pulled back the hammer on his gun with a loud click. "You told me that bird of yours couldn't lose."

"No, *señor*. I said he has never lost." The old man trembled as he began to stroke the head of the dead bird, and he looked up at Royce with watery eyes. Then, holding the bird gently, he struggled to his feet. "He has never lost—until now," he said, his voice barely audible.

Royce knocked the bird out of the old man's hands, sending it flying several feet into the air. It landed with a dull thud in the dust of the street. He grabbed the old man by his dirty, tattered shirt and pulled him close until their faces were only inches apart. "I want my money back," Royce hissed. "Do you hear me?"

The old peasant's trembling worsened as Royce threatened him again with his gun. "*Sí, señor,* I hear. But I have no money. I bet it all . . ." He glanced sorrowfully at the dead bird. Royce holstered his gun and struck him a savage blow with the back of his hand, instantly drawing blood from the old man's mouth, and prompting him to hold up his hands in a feeble gesture of defense. Royce drew his six-shooter again and pressed it against the elderly Mexican's temple.

"*Por favor, señor.* Please—I can do nothing."

The dusty plaza grew ominously silent. There were no more hushed whispers from the onlookers; no dogs barked; no horses snorted or stomped the ground. Royce's finger tightened around the trigger of his weapon.

"How'd you like to try that with someone who can fight back?" said a low voice from somewhere in the crowd.

Royce spun around, his knees flexed, his gun hand thrust forward. His eyes searched the frightened faces that lined the street. Then he saw the young cowboy. He was standing at the hitch rail in front of the cantina, feet apart, his hands on his hips. He was dressed in chaps, shirt, and vest, and wore a white Stetson pushed back from his handsome face. Royce guessed that he was about twenty-four or twenty-five years old.

"This any of your business?" Royce growled.

"It could be," the cowboy said, as he slowly lowered his right hand until it hung loosely at his hip, next to a holster decorated with a silver conch that glinted in the midday sun.

"You must like taking chances," Royce said, "shooting your mouth off to a man with a gun in his hand."

"I just thought maybe you should leave the old man alone." The cowboy moved toward the middle of the square. What remained of the crowd of men backed slowly toward the protection of the rickety buildings, while the few women among them herded their children off the street. One of the vaqueros who had been plying the heavy-drinking woman with liquor came out onto the steps of the cantina and stood watching. The cowboy stopped and planted his feet.

"Besides," he said, "I heard you were looking for me."

Royce studied the young man, taking careful note of the blond hair that sprouted from under his Stetson and the cold blue eyes that stared back, clear and steady. *Could this really be him?* Royce wondered. "Your name's Ward?" he said.

The cowboy nodded, his eyes never leaving Royce. "Yeah, I'm Ward."

"I'll get to you later." Royce reached down and jerked the old Mexican roughly to his feet. "Right now you're interfering with my business."

Ward started slowly in their direction. "I still think you should leave him alone."

Royce chuckled without humor. "And if I don't?" He put his gun to the old man's head again.

"Mister, don't do that." Ward's voice was still quiet, but now it was cold and edged with steel.

Royce pushed the old man down into the street again and turned to the cowboy. "You must be in a hurry to die."

The young man who claimed to be Ward raised his hand away from his holster. "I'm not looking for a fight. I just don't like to see people pushed around—especially when they can't push back." He walked to the old man and helped him up, then picked up the dead bird and handed it to him.

"*¡Cuidado!*" It was the voice of the vaquero. "Look out!"

The cowboy whirled, clutching for the iron on his hip. The roar of a gun was loud in the quiet street. Then Royce quickly scanned the crowd, his whole being filled with hatred for whoever had shouted the warning. His gaze came to rest on the vaquero. The man's face was as white as the sun-bleached adobe bricks of the building behind him, and his eyes widened in fear as Royce glared at him and slowly raised his gun and aimed it at his heart.

"Next time you interfere, I'll kill you too."

Revulsion replaced the fear in the young man's eyes as Royce holstered his .45 and walked casually back toward the cantina. And dust devils swirled around the body that lay in the street.

Chapter Two

Clay Archer sat astride his horse on a hillside over-looking a shallow valley. From his position in a stand of mesquite trees, he watched the three men on the valley floor less than two hundred yards away as they herded a dozen beef cattle into a makeshift holding pen made of split rails. One of the men stopped and pointed to something across the valley. Archer turned his gaze in the same direction just in time to see a momentary glint of light from somewhere in the trees on the opposite hillside. He dug a pair of binoculars out of his saddlebag and put them to his eyes.

As he traversed the ridgeline, Archer saw the flash again and he sharpened the focus in his glasses. Now he had a clear view of a mounted rider who sat partially concealed in the trees across the valley. Reflected sunlight bounced from something shiny on the holster that he wore on his right hip. Archer angled the glasses up to the man's face, and the breath caught in his chest, and he felt the hair rise on the back of his neck.

"Ward!" he hissed in disbelief. Archer took the glasses away from his face, rubbed his eyes, then looked again. "You're supposed to be dead," he said aloud, and he shivered as if he were watching a ghost.

In the valley, two cowboys tried to coax an obstinate steer, the last of a small herd, into a split-rail corral. One of the men glared at the third member of the group, who had turned in his saddle and sat staring at a clump of mesquite trees on the nearby hills. "We could use a little help here, Cassidy," the man said, "instead of you sittin' there daydreamin'."

"I ain't daydreamin', Jack," Cassidy said. "Didn't you see that?"

"See what?" Jack said gruffly as he finally got the last steer into the corral and closed the gate.

"Didn't you see somethin' shiny flashin' in the sun?" Cassidy pointed to the hillside. "See, there it is again. There's someone up there."

"Yeah, now I see him," Jack said and he pointed at the rider who was only partially visible in the dappled light that filtered through the branches of the mesquites dotting the nearby slopes. "Where's the light comin' from?" he said. "Is he holding a mirror or somethin'?"

"He's got something shiny on his holster," Cassidy answered.

"Who is it?" the third man said, and he moved his horse to Cassidy's side.

"Why're you askin' me?" Cassidy growled. "What do you think I am, some kind of mind reader?"

"What's he doin' up there?" Jack wanted to know.

Cassidy pulled a Winchester rifle out of the scabbard lashed to the side of his horse. "He's fixin' to git hisself killed, that's what," he answered, and levered a shell into the rifle's chamber.

"How come?" Jack asked. "He ain't doin' nothing but sittin' there."

"He's seen too much. The boss'll skin us alive if he finds out we let someone see us move them cows." Cassidy put the rifle to his shoulder and fired, and the slug clipped a tree branch just over the lone rider's head. He fired two more quick shots that raised plumes of dust at the feet of the rider's horse as he wheeled his mount and charged out of the clump of trees.

"Let's get him!" Cassidy barked, and spurred his horse into motion. His two companions followed, and they raced across the valley floor and started up the gentle slope of the hill. The fleeing rider turned in his saddle as he galloped across the ridgeline toward a stand of pine trees in the near distance, and the six-shooter in his hand belched smoke as he fired several quick shots at his pursuers.

The man riding on Cassidy's left clutched at his

shoulder, swayed dizzily in his saddle for a moment, grasping at the horn, then tumbled backwards over his horse's rump and thudded to the ground in a dusty heap. Cassidy kept the Winchester pressed to his shoulder and, controlling his racing mount with just his knees, squeezed off another series of shots while Jack blazed away with his .45.

"He's headin' for the dry wash," Cassidy yelled over the beat of pounding hooves, and he lowered his rifle and took up the reins again in his free hand. "Let's cut him off!" They turned their thundering horses toward the scrub pines and raced full tilt on a line intended to intercept the hard-riding stranger.

Justin Ward dropped his Colt revolver into its holster and leaned low over his saddle horn, his face practically touching his horse's neck. He jabbed his spurs firmly into the animal's flanks, then turned to glance over his shoulder. The riders were coming hard, closing fast. Ward spurred his horse again and pointed him in the direction of what appeared to be a faint trail leading into the scrubby trees before he chanced another look backward. His pursuers obviously knew the terrain and had taken a course that enabled them to cover ground quickly.

"Come on, boy," he whispered into his horse's flying mane as it whipped about his face. His breathing came faster now. "You've got to outrun these guys," he said, and trying to make himself as small a target as possible, he pressed his face tighter against the horse's lathered neck. He raced past the first of the pines and, over the clatter of pounding hooves, heard the bark of a Colt .45 and the crack of a Winchester, followed by the angry buzz of lead as it zipped through the branches near his head. "C'mon, fella," he whispered again to his straining mount, "we can lose 'em in these trees."

Following the vague trail, Ward plunged deeper into the thickening forest of pines, urging his horse to even greater speed. Now he could see that the trail ahead split into two poorly defined paths. With only an instant to make a decision, he reined the charging roan to the left and almost immediately regretted his choice. The level terrain suddenly gave way to a treacherous slope that led down a steep embankment to a dry streambed. He had no alternative but to rein his mount to a skidding, sliding stop or risk tumbling headlong into the gully below. But with the sound of pounding hoofbeats and the yells of his pursuers growing louder by the second, he knew what he had to do.

"Let's go, pal." He urged the reluctant animal into a stiff-legged, near-vertical plunge down the sandy embankment. "Good boy," Ward whispered as he reached the bottom of the wash. He patted the roan affectionately on the neck, then risked a quick look over his shoulder before starting up the opposite bank.

The two riders had reined up and seemed unsure whether or not they should chance the precipitous slope. The man with the rifle put it to his shoulder again, stirring Ward to coax more speed out of his gasping horse as he strained up the steep incline.

Just as they reached the upper crest of the wash, a shot rang out and Ward felt the impact of a 38.55 slug as it tore into his right shoulder, practically throwing him out of the saddle. With his right arm hanging useless now at his side, he grasped at the saddle horn with his left hand, and as he gained level ground he took another frantic look back at the riders.

To Ward's dismay, they had overcome their hesitation and were making their way carefully to the bottom of the wash. So with blood quickly soaking his shirtsleeve, he again put spurs to his horse's flanks and, feeling relieved to be back on level ground, galloped toward what he hoped would be an escape route through the scrub pine. But his relief vanished with the crack of another rifle shot. In the same instant Ward felt like he had been kicked in the head by a pair of mules, and the skin along his left temple burned as if seared by a white-hot branding iron. He was suddenly dizzy, not sure how much longer he could stay in the saddle, and he guided his pounding horse toward a thicket of creosote bushes sprouting among the pines.

Now his eyes kept slipping in and out of focus, and

Ward realized there was no chance he could outrun his tormentors. As he burst into the cluster of greasewoods, momentarily out of sight of the riders behind him, he reined up abruptly and, with his strength rapidly ebbing, slid to the ground. He took off his hat and struck his horse a sharp blow to the rump and, with the aid of a throaty yell, startled the animal into a gallop out of the thicket. As the horse raced away, Ward could hear the sound of other pounding hooves rapidly growing louder. He summoned his last reserves of strength and threw himself into the closest tangle of pine and greasewood, hoping it would offer him concealment from the fast-approaching cowboys. But now the loss of blood and the blow to the head took their toll, and he felt himself sinking into a dark, swirling abyss. About to lose consciousness, he was barely aware of the two straining, sweating horses thundering by and a voice that called out, "There he goes! I just seen him cut through those trees!"

Then there was nothing but blackness.

Ward had no idea how long he had been unconscious—or even what had happened or where he was. All he knew for the moment was that his head throbbed like it was going to explode and there was no feeling in his right arm. He ran his tongue over sandpaper lips and thought about how good a drink of cool water would taste about now. Feeling as if someone was banging a Chinese gong inside his skull, he struggled into a sitting position and rested his back against a fallen tree trunk.

Wisps of memory began to compete with the hammering in his brain, and he put his good hand to his lifeless arm. The shirtsleeve was sodden and sticky. He probed his shoulder gingerly and his fingers came away shiny with fresh blood. Now the memory of the cowboys, and the brief chase through the hillside and the dry wash filled his mind and helped drive out the pain in his head and ease the ache that had started in his shoulder.

Ward was lightheaded and realized he had to stop the flow of blood that still oozed from the rifle wound before he became so weak he wouldn't be able to move. He didn't relish the idea of slowly bleeding to death among the scrubby pines and creosote bushes. Only able to use his left hand, he struggled to undo the large bandanna at his neck, and by holding one end in his teeth, he managed to tie it tightly around his bloody shirt over the wound. After a few minutes, he decided he had to risk trying to stand up, so with the aid of a nearby tree branch he staggered to his feet as waves of dizziness swept over him. The gong player hammered out a new, throbbing cadence, and Ward was afraid he would pass out again. But after several minutes the pounding in his head lessened and he chanced a few halting steps to where his hat lay in the dirt. Now he remembered driving off his beautiful roan and wondered if he would ever see the magnificent animal again.

But he would have to cope with that problem later. Holding his aching shoulder, Ward forced himself to take one painful step after another along the hint of a trail he had seen from the other side of the wash. He had no idea where it would lead, but for now it was the only chance he had to survive. And if he didn't find help soon, even that chance would be lost to him.

From his seat in the driver's box of the swaying stagecoach, Harv Ferguson snapped the reins over the backs of the four-horse team. "Eeeyah!" he yelled, as dust roiling up from the hooves of the racing animals swirled around him and filled his eyes and nostrils and even his mouth whenever he tried to spit a stream of tobacco juice over the side of the coach. All he wanted now was to get to town and have a big, cold glass of beer, and maybe even a bath—but there was no hurry about that last part.

He glanced at Charlie Simms, dozing in the seat beside him, his shotgun cradled loosely in the crook of one arm. Harv wondered how the grizzled old man could sleep in the swaying, jouncing coach—and in the dust.

Something in the brush along the road ahead caught Harv's eye, and he blinked and ran a gloved hand over his face. There was a flash of light like the reflection from a mirror. Then through the waves of shimmering heat rising from the trail he saw a man step out of the brush. Actually, to say that he staggered out was more like it. Harv wondered if maybe he was drunk. But no matter what he was, this was an odd place for a man on foot. He prodded his companion with an elbow.

"Wake up, Charlie!"

The old shotgun rider bolted upright, lips smacking and eyes like saucers. "Wha . . . what in blazes is goin' on?" Harv pointed. "So?" Charlie growled. "There's a feller standin' alongside the road. You woke me up for that?" He rubbed the sleep from his eyes and squinted. "It kind of looks like he might be hurt."

"It could be a trick," Harv replied.

"That ain't likely. Everybody 'round here knows we don't carry nothin' worth robbin'. I say he must be hurt."

"Okay, okay, I'm goin' to stop," Harv said, "but you just keep that scattergun handy." He pulled the horses to a gradual halt and yelled down to the couple of passengers who had poked their heads out the window. "We'll only be a minute, folks. Just stay inside."

The man staggered out onto the dirt road and weaved unsteadily toward the coach. "Been shot," he said hoarsely, and stopped by the front wheel, steadying himself with one hand while his other arm hung uselessly at his side.

"Where're you headed?" Charlie asked.

"Wherever you are," he replied weakly.

"Hold on there, bub," Harv barked, eying the stranger with suspicion. "Who are you, and where do you come from?"

The man slumped against the wheel, clearly in danger of falling. "Can't you see he needs help?" Charlie said. He laid the shotgun on the seat and began to climb down from the coach. But before he could reach the ground, the wounded man's knees buckled and, as if his bones had turned to rubber, he collapsed like a pile of dirty clothes onto the rutted trail.

Chapter Three

A hand-painted sign over the front door of a two-story frame building read *General Store, Milt Wells, Proprietor.* Mary Wells was sweeping off the board sidewalk that ran past the store and continued along a main street lined with mostly false-front clapboard buildings and an occasional adobe brick structure that broke up the monotony.

At the sound of the afternoon stage, Mary stopped sweeping and looked toward the end of the street as the coach rolled in from the open range and turned toward the center of town. A few people along the sidewalk stopped to watch as it clattered over the wagon ruts in the near-empty street and came to a straining, squealing stop at the Overland office building that stood next to the general store. A couple of barefoot boys appeared out of nowhere and stood fidgeting and grinning at the prospects of helping the passengers with their valises in hopes of some small reward.

Mary began to sweep halfheartedly again at the

couple of wooden steps that led from the sidewalk down to the street, glancing up occasionally to watch the driver hand down some cartons to Charlie, along with a couple of carpet bags from the roof of the coach. Then Charlie opened the passenger door and, much to the delight of the waiting boys, two men stepped out. Dressed in suits and bowler hats, they looked like drummers, or maybe gamblers, come to ply their game at the Red Dog Saloon across the street. They moved stiffly but quickly to their valises, picked them up and strode away, leaving the boys crestfallen. Mary smiled sympathetically as they jammed their hands in their pockets and, shoulders sagging, slouched down the street.

Then another man appeared in the open doorway.

He wore a gun on his hip, the holster tied down to his leg. Mary stopped sweeping. Men like this rarely came to Purgatory. After all, it was just a cow town. A few stores, a blacksmith shop, one bank, a telegraph office, Hennessey's restaurant, and a livery stable. It was just the kind of town that took care of the needs of the local ranchers. And of course there was a jail and a sheriff, not that he had much to do most of the time, except for an occasional fight in the saloon—or so Mary had heard. She had never been in the place.

She eyed the stranger who was still standing in the open door of the coach, partly hidden in shadow. He wasn't so much standing as he was slumping, holding the door frame with one hand while his other hand hung limply at his side. Her gaze was drawn to the gun on his hip and the fancy holster with some kind of silver decoration on it. Mary hated guns, and the violence that usually accompanied them. Suddenly she was glad there was a sheriff in town.

Charlie looked up at him. "You need help gettin' down, young fella?"

The man didn't answer but, with his face twisted in a grimace, stepped gingerly from the coach. He stood for a moment, holding the door frame, while he surveyed the street from one end to the other. His eyes came to rest on Mary. They were blue and cold. Mary thought they were filled with suspicion. She shuddered when he stared at her, and felt the heat rise in her cheeks as he looked her up and down brazenly. Then she saw his bloody shirt, the dusty hat that hung down his back by a leather thong, and his blond hair that was crusted over his left ear and stuck to his scalp—and she wondered what kind of a man this could be.

"You don't look so hot, mister," Charlie said, and put a gentle hand on the wounded man's good shoulder. "You got friends in town? You got a place to stay?"

The man acted like he didn't hear. He touched his fingers to the wound on his head and winced, then gazed around blankly. "You goin' to be okay?" Charlie said, his hand still on the man's shoulder.

"Yeah," he growled and pushed Charlie's hand away, "don't worry about it."

Charlie shrugged. "Suit yourself." Then he climbed back into the seat and the driver snapped the reins over his team and the coach pulled away.

Mary watched as the stranger, alone now in the street, took a couple of halting steps, then paused. She was both fascinated and repulsed by his appearance. His face, though etched with pain, was undeniably handsome; but with the terrible gun on his hip and his bloody wounds he exuded pure violence.

Mary shivered again. She knew she should be afraid of this man, but at the same time she could see he needed help. "Are you . . . ?" she started weakly. "Is there . . . is there anything I can do . . . ?"

He took a step in her direction and, without warning, crumpled to the street.

"Oh, good heavens!" Mary dropped her broom and ran to him. She stood with a hand pressed to her mouth, not sure what to do. Passersby on the sidewalk slowed to look; a few stopped, then moved on. Mary searched the faces of the small crowd that began to form. "Won't somebody help me with this man?" No one moved. An old woman stopped on the sidewalk in front of the store and, pointing her long nose in the air, glared down at Mary.

"This is absolutely disgusting!" the woman said.

"Imagine parading around drunk in the middle of the day!"

"He's hardly parading—can't you see he's hurt?" Mary said, glaring back, suddenly feeling a twinge of sympathy for the wounded man who lay helpless at her feet.

The old woman stalked off, snorting indignantly, and the small crowd began to drift away.

Hesitantly, tentatively, Mary put a hand to the man's forehead, careful not to touch the mass of crusted blood. His skin felt like it was on fire, as though he was being consumed by fever, and his breath was coming in quick, shallow gasps. She was about to call for help again when she saw Matt Hennessey appear in the doorway of a small shingled building that was wedged between the general store and telegraph office.

Hennessey was in shirtsleeves, and his ample waist was covered by a white apron that reached nearly to his boot tops. He stood for a minute under a sign that read *Hennessey's Restaurant, World-Famous Irish Stew*, and when he saw Mary his forehead twisted into a worried frown. "Mary," he yelled, "what happened?" and he stepped into the street and waddled quickly in her direction. When he got to her side he knelt next to the unconscious man. "Is he alive?" he asked in his thick brogue. Then, as if to answer his own question, he pressed his fingers to the man's neck, feeling for a pulse. "Just barely," he whispered to himself.

"Oh, Matt," Mary said, "thank you. No one else would even consider . . ."

A wide smile split the Irishman's ruddy face, and his emerald eyes flashed. "He might be a customer for some of me stew. I couldn't see just lettin' him lay here in the street." Then his look grew serious. "But he looks like he's in pretty bad shape."

"I know," Mary replied. "I think we have to get him inside." She ran to the steps in front of the general store and yelled through the open door. "Dad, will you give us a hand, please?"

Within seconds, a tall, plain-looking man appeared in the doorway. Under a shock of graying hair, his face was a mixture of curiosity and concern. He was dressed in black pants and a white shirt with sleeve garters around his arms and a string tie at his neck. "What's going on, Mary?" he said as he followed his daughter back into the street and stood looking down at the stranger. "Who is this man?"

"I don't know, Dad. He just arrived on the stage. All I know is that he's badly hurt."

"Howdy, Milt," Hennessey said, glancing up at the storekeeper.

"What are we going to do?" Mary asked, looking into her father's gentle gray eyes.

"Help me get him inside, Matt," he said to Hennessey and knelt beside the Irishman. Together they raised the nearly unconscious man slowly to his feet, a move that caused him to wince and groan softly. "We'll put him on that bunk in the back room," Milt said as he and Matt eased the man up the steps and into the dimness of the general store.

Though the day was warm, Mary hugged herself for just an instant as a shiver ran along her spine. She wasn't sure she liked the idea of having this man under her roof. But she was sure of one thing—she didn't like having that terrible gun around. She would have to talk to her father about it when the time was right. Then the sound of a door closing somewhere put the thought out of her mind and she turned to see Sheriff Travis Dutton leave the jail and start across the street toward the telegraph office.

He smiled at Mary and touched a hand to his hat brim. She smiled back, feeling a little embarrassed. She knew Travis was fond of her, maybe too fond since she didn't feel the same affection for him.

"Howdy, Mary."

"Hello, Travis," Mary said and nodded in the sheriff's direction.

He stopped at the telegraph office door. "I see you've got a new boarder."

Mary thought there was a note of criticism in the sheriff's voice, and for a moment it annoyed her. She didn't know what to say so she just nodded again. Travis opened the door and stood with his hand on the latch. "Make sure you keep a sharp eye out. And tell Milt he's got to be careful takin' in strangers like that."

"I'm sure he'll appreciate the advice," Mary said, still feeling a little testy. She didn't like Travis telling her what to do, whether he was the sheriff or not.

"Tell him I'll be in to see him in a day or so—soon's I make some inquiries." Then Travis touched his hat again and stepped into the telegraph office and closed the door behind him.

A breeze ruffled the skirt of Mary's dress, and she felt a chill as she walked quickly toward the general store.

Clay Archer guided his horse through a stand of cottonwoods toward a decrepit line shack that was partially concealed in the trees. The thin curl of smoke drifting lazily up from the stovepipe that stuck out through the curled, sun-bleached shingles of the roof, and the three horses tied up at the rail, assured him that the men he was looking for were inside. He reined up at the front of the shack and dismounted.

Archer paused for a moment before going in, listening to the muffled sound of voices. Then he pushed open the door and stepped inside. Cassidy and Jack, the men who had chased Ward through the dry wash, were standing by a small cast-iron stove. A third cowboy was seated at a rough table; he had one arm in a sling made from his bandanna, and a dirty bandage showed under the open collar of his shirt. All the men had tin mugs in their hands, and when they saw Archer they abruptly stopped talking.

"Howdy, boss," Cassidy said finally, grinning awkwardly. "What are you doin' out here? We thought you was back at the ranch." He went to the stove before Archer could reply and reached for the dented coffee pot. "How 'bout some java?"

Archer ignored his offer. "That all you saddle bums got to do—hang around drinkin' coffee?"

Cassidy pointed to the wounded cowboy. "Old Billy here accidentally caught a slug in his shoulder . . ."

"Yeah, and I know how he got it," Archer snarled. "And it wasn't no accident." The other three were suddenly wide-eyed. "It was three against one," Archer continued, his voice heavy with contempt. "How could you let him get away?"

"Who're you talking about?" Cassidy said, looking sheepish.

"Don't give me any of that *who* business," Archer shot back. "I'm talkin' about the man that saw you movin' them steers, that's who."

Cassidy's mouth dropped open.

"You didn't know I was watching, did you?" Archer

said. The three men exchanged guilty looks. "Well, I was. So how'd you let him get away?"

"He's good, Clay," Cassidy said, and hung his head and stared into his coffee, "real good."

"No one's that good," Archer growled.

"Cassidy plugged him for sure," Jack volunteered with a hopeful grin on his face. "He can't get far."

"Then why ain't you dumbbells out there lookin' for him right now instead of standin' around here?"

"Well," Cassidy started lamely, "we had to see to Billy. I didn't think . . ."

"Think!" Archer roared. "What in tarnation have you got to think with, any of you? If you could think, you'd've never let him get a look at them steers in the first place!"

"Come on, Clay," Billy said. "He don't know for sure we rustled that beef."

"No," Archer shot back, "but that's what old man Kelso's payin' him to find out."

"You know who that guy is?" Cassidy said, a surprised look on his slow-witted face.

"His name's Ward," Archer said. "He's supposed to be dead. Story is he was killed down in Mexico. But now, if he gets to the U.S. marshal, we could all wind up as decorations on a tree limb."

"We'll find him, Clay," Cassidy insisted, and pointed

at the wounded cowboy. "We just had to get old Billy patched up, and then we'll be back on the trail. We'll find him."

"You couldn't find your hat on your head," Archer growled. "The three of you get back to the ranch before the old man wonders where you are."

"Don't you want . . . ?" Cassidy started.

"I don't want you numskulls to do anything. You've made enough of a mess out of things as it is. Unless I miss my guess, Ward's halfway to Mexico by now. Just get back to the ranch. I'll handle this myself."

Chapter Four

T ravis Dutton left the telegraph office and started back
toward the jail. Halfway across the street he changed his
mind and headed for Hennessey's restaurant. It was time
for a cup of coffee. Travis didn't like the Irishman very
much; he was always bragging about how good his cooking was, especially his stew. Dutton thought it was awful.
But he did like Hennessey's coffee. It was a lot better than
he could ever get out of the grimy old pot he kept on the
stove back at the jail.

"Top of the mornin' to you, Sheriff," Hennessey said
as Dutton came into the restaurant and took a seat at the
counter. Though the greeting seemed pleasant enough,
it lacked any real warmth. Dutton knew that Hennessey
was not exactly one of his admirers, although he wasn't
sure why. He couldn't remember ever causing the Irishman any trouble—not that he had thought much about
it one way or the other.

"What can I get you?" Hennessey asked.

"I'll have coffee."

While Hennessey poured the brew, two men farther along the counter nodded to the sheriff without speaking, then went back to their whispered conversation.

"We were just talkin' about you, Sheriff," Hennessey said as he set the steaming mug on the counter.

"Yeah? What were you saying about me?"

"Well, we weren't talking about you exactly, but about that man that came in on the stage nearly a week ago, all shot up."

"What about him?"

"That's what we were wonderin'. Him wearin' a fancy rig and all, we wondered if he might be somebody . . ."

"Yeah, Sheriff," one of the men at the counter said, "story is he looked like he could be some kind of gun hand. But no one's seen hide nor hair of him since Milt Wells took him in. Some people are getting a little nervous about havin' a man like that in town."

Dutton snorted. "Like who—a bunch of old ladies? You let me take care of that stranger. I been makin' some inquiries. I should hear back any day now. Meantime, I got my eye on things."

The other man at the counter said, "And there's been a lot of talk around town lately about cattle rustlin' out at the Kelso place. We wondered if this fella might have somethin' to do with it. Maybe you ought to . . ."

"What talk about rustlin'? I ain't heard any talk about

rustlin' at the Kelso spread." Dutton slurped at his coffee.

The man at the counter frowned and gave Hennessey a quick look. "You must be the only one," he said to Dutton. "It's all over town."

"I think I ought to know," Dutton snarled. "Clay Archer's a good friend of mine. He's been the ramrod for the Kelso brand for nearly ten years. If there was any rustlin' goin' on he'd've told me about it."

"That's strange," Hennessey said as he offered Dutton more coffee, "you not hearin' any of the talk."

The sheriff waved off the coffee pot and scowled.

"No matter," Hennessey went on, "we just thought this was somethin' you might want to look into—this stranger, I mean."

Dutton stood up and gave Hennessey a dark look. "I don't need no hash slinger tellin' me how to do my job. I'll take care of this stranger in my own way and in my own time."

"No offense, Sheriff." Hennessey picked up the dirty mug and wiped at the counter. "But a lot of folks are a little nervous about havin' this man in town—that plus the rustlin'. I just thought you'd like to know."

Dutton tossed a coin on the counter and stalked out of the restaurant.

"Hand me those blankets there, will you, Mary?"

Milt Wells was standing on a stool rearranging stock

on one of the shelves at the front of the general store. While he waited for Mary to pass him the blankets he glanced out the window just in time to see Travis Dutton come out of Hennessey's restaurant. "Looks like the sheriff's heading this way," Milt said as Mary passed up the folded blankets. "Wonder what's on his mind."

"I could guess," Mary said and stood looking out the window as the sheriff approached.

"It's a little early in the day to come courting, don't you think?" Milt said, and smiled as the color rose in his daughter's cheeks.

"Oh, Dad, don't be silly. If I had to guess, I'd say he's coming to talk to you about our guest in the storeroom."

"We'll know in a minute," Milt said, and stepped down from the stool just as Dutton reached the front door. "Morning, Travis," he said as the sheriff came in and made his way toward the counter where Mary was standing.

"Mornin'," Dutton said absently, not even bothering to look at the storekeeper. He smiled at Mary and swept off his Stetson, revealing a thick head of dark brown hair that fell nearly to his shoulders. "Howdy, Mary," he said, and stood fingering the brim of his hat. "You're lookin' pert this mornin'."

"Good morning, Travis," Mary replied. "What brings you around so early?"

"I was wondering the same thing," Milt said as he walked to where the two were standing, "if I'm not intruding, that is." He grinned.

The sheriff looked surprised. "What? Oh, of course not, Milt." Travis smiled lamely. "Sorry, I didn't mean to . . . I was just gettin' to that." He paused for a moment, looking awkward, then said, "You still got that stranger in your back room?"

"As a matter of fact, we do," Milt replied. "And from the looks of things, he's likely to be there for a spell."

Travis frowned and his look grew somber. "I'd like to have a talk with him."

"So would I," Milt said.

"If he ever wakes up long enough, maybe we can," Mary added. "All he does is sleep—and maybe eat once in a while."

The furrows in Travis' brow deepened, and he looked intently into her eyes. "You be careful around him, Mary." He put a lingering, protective hand on her arm.

Mary withdrew from his touch. "Thank you, Sheriff," she said testily, her eyes snapping. "I can take care of myself."

"But you don't know anything about this man."

"How about you, Sheriff?" Milt wanted to know. "Have you ever seen him before? Do you have any idea who he is?"

"I been through all the wanted posters over at the

jail," Dutton said, and went back to fingering his hat. "I got nothin' on anyone that fits his description—what I seen of him, that is. I didn't get too good a look at him that day he got off the stage. Maybe if I could . . ." He nodded toward the storeroom door.

"Not just yet," Milt said. "Give it a few more days. He's not going anywhere."

Dutton shrugged. "Anyway, I wired the marshal's office in Tucson but ain't heard back yet. I was just over to the telegraph office a while ago. It might take a few more days." He put a hand on Mary's arm again. "You just be careful, you hear?"

"Don't worry so much," Mary said, more gently this time, and stepped away from Dutton's reach.

"I'll be sure to be careful too," Milt said, unable to hold back a slight smile, "in case you're interested."

Travis blushed under his tanned face and worried the brim of his hat with renewed vigor. "I just meant that . . ."

"I know," Milt said and allowed himself a chuckle.

Dutton put on his hat and, with his face still showing color, started for the door. "Just let me know when he comes to long enough for me to talk to him."

"We'll do that, Sheriff," Milt said, still smiling as Dutton strode out the door. Then he turned to his daughter. "Looks like Travis could be a mite jealous."

"Of what?" Mary said, her eyebrows arching.

"Oh, I don't know, but that stranger's a mighty good-looking young fellow."

"Oh, fiddlesticks!" Mary said and went back to folding blankets. After a moment she paused and turned to her father, her face drawn into a slight scowl. "But the sheriff's right, you know. We do have to be careful."

Clay Archer sat easy in the saddle as he loped past a faded sign at the side of a street lined with an odd assortment of wood and adobe buildings. Though the sign said *Nogales, Arizona Terr.*, the street felt and looked like it could have been in Mexico. It even sounded like it. The bits of conversation that Archer overheard from the people he rode past were in Spanish as often as in English. The place even smelled Mexican, with the odor of baking tortillas and pungent cooking oil wafting from the open food stalls that beckoned to hungry passersby.

As Archer approached the largest building in view, the street sounds gave way to the discordant notes of a piano being played badly, and yelps and hoots of laughter. He reined up under a colorful sign that boldly identified the Good Time Saloon, dismounted, walked up two wooden steps, and pushed through a set of swinging doors.

The saloon was true to its name. Cigar smoke hung like a gauze curtain over a room nearly filled with rowdy cowboys and painted women. Two bartenders, looking frazzled, strained to keep up with the riotous crowd's demands for whiskey and tequila. A man in a bowler hat and with sleeve garters on his arms pounded away at an upright piano, but his playing was weak competition for the yells and laughter and the rumble of raucous conversation.

Archer scanned the men along the bar, then turned his attention to the three poker tables in the middle of the room. They were all filled. Serious-faced men smoked, drank, and held their cards close to their vests. Then he saw Royce. He was at the table farthest from the door, his cards facedown in front of him and his fingers toying with a stack of coins. His cold eyes revealed nothing. A young girl, her obviously once-pretty face rendered grotesque by too much rouge and powder, stood at Royce's side with one slender, bare arm resting on his shoulder. He looked up as Archer approached the table, a raised eyebrow the only hint of surprise.

"Ward's alive," Archer said, just loud enough to be heard over the noise. "We need to talk." Royce stared back without speaking, as though trying to decide whether or not Archer was serious.

He tossed his cards into the pile of money in the center of the table. "I'm out," he said, then stood up, retrieved his stack of coins, and headed across the room with Archer close on his heels. "Have a drink?" Royce said when they reached the bar and, without waiting for an answer, signaled for one of the bartenders. "Give us a bottle," he said when the sweating man approached, "and two glasses."

"You owe me, Royce," Archer said after the bartender left the whiskey and glasses. Royce ignored the comment and poured himself a drink and sipped at it slowly. "Did you hear what I said? Ward's alive." Archer grabbed Royce by the elbow in an attempt to get his attention. "You owe me!"

Royce turned slowly. His eyes were mere slits, but filled with such evil that Archer was suddenly afraid. Royce's hand shot out like a striking snake and gripped Archer's wrist and squeezed until it felt like he would break the bones. "Don't you ever put your hands on me again," he hissed, and slammed Archer's arm down with such force that the bottle and glasses danced on the bar. Then, after he finished his drink, he said, "Now, what's this about Ward?"

"He's still alive," Archer said, trying to hide the fear in his voice. "That's why you owe . . ."

"I owe you nothing," Royce insisted. "I killed him in Mexico."

"Then it was his ghost I seen three days ago, not thirty miles from here."

"That's your problem," Royce replied, his voice flat, devoid of emotion, displaying his complete lack of concern.

Archer reached for the bottle and, with a slight tremble

in his hand, poured himself a drink. "He caught my boys movin' some steers. They winged him, but he got away." He took a quick swallow of whiskey, hoping it would help stop his trembling. "I figure he might've headed back to Mexico."

"Why would he do that?"

"I think he knows that's where we sell that rustled beef. He was down there nosin' around. That's why I sent you down there lookin' for him in the first place."

"And that's where I found him." Royce poured more whiskey in his glass. "So what do you want from me?"

"I want Ward dead."

"It'll cost you," Royce said and downed his drink.

"I paid you once!" Archer protested.

"And I did the job." Royce shrugged. It was plain that, as far as he was concerned, there was nothing more to discuss. Archer opened his mouth to argue but changed his mind. Royce had him over a barrel. If he said he killed Ward there was no way for Archer to prove that he didn't. Except he knew what he had seen, and he had seen Ward alive. But he was afraid of Royce; the man was a ruthless killer, fast with a gun. He gulped down the last of his whiskey, then said, "All right. Just see that you finish the job this time."

Ward opened his eyes and looked around the room. He had the strange feeling he had seen it before, then realized he had been drifting in and out of consciousness for . . . how long had it been? He couldn't remember. The place looked like some kind of storeroom. There were crates and cartons and barrels stacked against two walls, and what appeared to be an old chest of drawers stood in one corner next to a window that looked out onto a narrow street, what he could see of it. And there were two doors in the room, one obviously leading to the outside and another leading . . . Ward didn't know where it led.

He tried to sit up in his narrow bunk. The effort sent a sharp pain through his right shoulder, and when he reached to determine what was causing the discomfort he realized that his upper arm was covered by a clean, neat bandage. The pain brought back the memory of the two riders and the impact of the rifle bullet that had nearly knocked him out of the saddle. Now he remembered the other shot that had creased his head, and he felt along his left temple; it, too, was covered with a bandage. Then, suddenly tired, he leaned back against the two pillows propped behind him.

Just as he was about to doze off, he heard voices coming from whatever lay behind the second door, and growing louder. It opened, and a young woman stepped into the room, a cautious, tentative look on her pretty face. She smiled when she saw that he was awake. "Well, well, if it isn't Lazarus," she said, her smile growing wider and her brown eyes shining.

Ward failed to see the humor in her greeting. "What's that supposed to mean?"

"It means that you've been either asleep or unconscious for the better part of a week," she answered as she walked farther into the room. She was followed by an older man, and though he had a kind face, Ward was immediately suspicious. He wondered who these people were. And as his hand moved instinctively to his right hip he was rewarded by another stab of pain. Now, for the first time, he realized he was naked in the bed except for the bottoms of his long johns, and he wondered what had happened to his gun as well as to his clothes.

"We were beginning to worry whether you were ever going to wake up," the woman said as she stood by the edge of the bunk.

"Where is . . . where are my things?" Ward wanted to know, his suspicion mounting.

She motioned toward the battered bureau. "Your clothes are in there—what there is left. I washed most of them, but I had to throw out your shirt. It had too much blood and dirt on it."

Ward scowled. He didn't like the idea of someone just throwing out his things without his say-so. He glared at the woman for several seconds, and her smile faded. "That's all right," she said, her tone growing cool, "you can thank me later." To his surprise she began to fluff up the pillows at his back and straighten out the blankets on the bunk. She had a clean, fresh smell about her, like a shirt that had been washed in strong soap and hung in the clear air to dry. He thought about how different she smelled from the dancehall girls he had known with their cheap perfume.

"Unless you'd prefer we call you Lazarus," she said while she worked, "you might want to tell us your name."

Ward grew cautious again. He wasn't about to tell strangers anything about himself. The woman finished straightening up the bunk and said, "You do have a name?"

He turned his head toward the window and looked out at the street. One of the buildings had an open front and was fitted with a forge and an anvil and a variety of tongs and hammers hanging from pegs in the wall. The words *Blacksmith and Livery Stable* were just barely legible on a smudged sign that hung over the opening.

"I said do you have a name?" The woman's voice was teasing, but persistent.

"Yeah," Ward answered, turning away from the window. "Sure, it's . . . my name's Livery—John Livery."

The man, who had been standing just inside the door, moved to the side of the bunk and spoke for the first time. "Nice to meet you, John Livery." He held out a hand and Ward responded awkwardly, not used to shaking with his left hand. The man had a firm, confident grip, and in spite of Ward's tendency to distrust strangers, he was surprised at the warmth he sensed in the handshake. "I'm Milt Wells," he said, "and this is my daughter, Mary. We run the general store, which, in case you haven't figured it out by now, is where you are."

"How long have I been here?"

"Oh, not long," Milt said, smiling, "several days."

"How'd I get here?" Ward had only vague recollections of what had happened to him after he ran his horse off in the pines and greasewoods.

"The afternoon stage," Milt said. "Harv Ferguson found you on the side of the road about five miles outside of town. You were in pretty bad shape. After Hennessey and I got you inside, Mary here cleaned your wounds and bandaged you up."

"Who's Hennessey?"

"He runs a restaurant in town. I suspect you'll get to meet him one of these days."

Ward glanced at Mary and she nodded and smiled thinly. Then he remembered he was practically naked. "Who changed . . . that is, who undressed me?"

Mary looked suddenly embarrassed; she blushed.

"Don't worry about that," Milt said. "The main thing is you're looking a whole lot better than the day we carried you in from the street."

"Are you hungry?" Mary asked.

Ward was suddenly ravenous. The thought of food made his stomach grumble. "I could eat," he said coolly, not wanting to acknowledge his eagerness.

"And you'll be able to manage by yourself, I hope," Mary said with a teasing twinkle in her eyes. "I'm getting a little tired of trying to feed you." She and her father exchanged smiles, but Ward just frowned. He had no memory of being fed. "There's some soup left from noon," she added.

"Then I guess it'll have to do," Ward said gruffly, annoyed to learn that he had been dependent on a woman for his feeding.

Mary's smile faded and the twinkle in her eyes was replaced by a cool stare. "I'm sure it will," she said brusquely. "Especially since you asked so nicely," she added, and turned on her heel and strode from the room.

Milt looked a little awkward and examined his fingers for a moment. "Sorry she got a little huffy there, John. But she's been working pretty hard taking care of you—though you might not know it."

Ward felt a twinge of remorse for his lack of gratitude but was in no mood to apologize. Instead he said, "You take in every beat-up stranger that comes to town?"

"There's no doctor here," Milt explained, "so we do the best we can."

Ward wondered if Milt and his daughter could really be that kind—and that willing to take unnecessary chances. "That could be dangerous," he said.

Milt shrugged. "I suppose," he replied and his look softened as he met Ward's gaze, "but the Good Samaritan took a chance. I figure I'm called to do at least as much."

Before Ward could answer, Mary swept into the room carrying a tray set with a bowl of soup and bread and eating utensils. "Help him sit up, will you please, Dad?" Her tone was still frosty. Milt fixed Ward's pillows and helped him get higher in the bunk while Mary put the food tray on his lap. The odor of the hot soup filled Ward's nostrils, and his belly grumbled again.

"I know it's not much," Mary said, a stern look on her face, "but it beats starving."

"Look," Ward said, "thanks. I'm sorry I was . . . Anyway, I'm sorry."

Mary's look softened, and a little of the sparkle came back into her eyes. "Eat your soup while it's hot," she said, then turned to her father. "Come on, Dad, let's leave him be so he can eat." She ushered Milt toward the door. "I'll be back for the tray later," she said, and they left Ward alone in the room.

He picked up the spoon with his right hand and reached for the steaming liquid. The sharp pain in his shoulder caused him to wince, and he set the spoon on the tray and lay back against the pillows. A twinge of uneasiness began somewhere deep in his gut, and he broke into a sweat that he knew wasn't because of the soup. *If I can't even lift a spoon,* he thought, *how can I handle a gun?* And he wondered if the men who shot him were still looking for him. "Guess I'll just have to be John Livery for a while," he whispered to the empty room, and picked up the spoon in his left hand.

Chapter Five

Mary glanced at John Livery out of the corner of her eye; she didn't want him to know she was watching. With his right arm still in a sling, he was struggling to fold a blanket on the counter in the main room of the general store, and she knew his awkwardness embarrassed and frustrated him. He had been working around the store for nearly three weeks now, and although Mary knew that his wounds were healing nicely and that he was regaining the use of his right hand, she also knew the pace of his recovery was far too slow as far as he was concerned.

She thought about how good he looked in the clean clothes her father had provided for him and how much more she liked seeing him with a storekeeper's apron tied around his waist rather than the frightful gun he was wearing the first time she saw him. Yet Mary found it curious that he had never asked about his gun—or anything else, for that matter—ever since he had gotten back on his feet and her father had offered him a job in the store.

But she had the feeling he knew where it was, wrapped up in a cloth and stuffed in the bottom drawer of the old bureau in the storeroom where she had put it the day he came to town. And somehow the fact that he never mentioned the gun bothered Mary. It was as though she wanted him to talk about it so she could tell him how she felt—how she hated guns and the violence they bred. Yet she didn't know why she should care whether or not he knew how she felt; after all, he was just a stranger waiting to get well enough to move on. Or at least that's what she told herself.

She glanced in Livery's direction again just as a blanket slipped from his hands and fell in a crumpled heap at his feet. Try as she might, Mary couldn't help but giggle at the woeful expression on his face. He turned toward her, anger and frustration plain in his look. Then his shoulders sagged and, to Mary's surprise, a thin, wry smile crossed his lips and he just stood shaking his head.

"Look," Mary said, "it's not your fault you can't do things with one hand." She went to him and stooped to retrieve the blanket. "When your arm gets better . . ." she started, just as he reached for the blanket at the same time. Their hands touched for an instant, and Mary felt a shiver of excitement she couldn't explain.

His deep blue eyes held her gaze for a moment, then he scowled. "When it's better," he said gruffly, "I'll be gone."

"You'll be gone where? You said you can't remember where you came from."

Livery reached for another blanket and tried to line up its folds. This one also fell to the floor, and he kicked at it viciously. "That's my problem."

"Well, you don't have to bite my head off. It might help if you tried not to be so ornery."

He stood for a moment, his head bowed and his eyes averted. "I'm not cut out to be a storekeeper," he grumbled.

"How do you know? You told us you don't remember what you used to do."

He picked up the blanket and tossed it on the counter. Then, without answering Mary's question, he turned and stalked across the room and went into the storeroom and slammed the door behind him.

"Are you having trouble?"

Mary turned to see her father come in the front door. He walked to her side, a questioning look on his face. "You and Mr. Livery aren't hitting it off too well?"

"I don't know," she said. "Sometimes he seems like he's almost trying to be friendly, then . . ."

Milt put an arm around her shoulders. "We need to be patient. Sometimes it takes a while to get over a head injury . . . to get your memory back."

"And if he never lost it, then what?" Mary said, not really knowing why she asked the question.

"You think he never lost it? That's nonsense. Of course he lost his memory. Why, he doesn't . . ."

"He remembers his name," Mary argued.

"Yes, but he's never so much as asked about his horse—or his gun. He obviously doesn't remember that he ever had . . ."

"I'm not so sure," Mary persisted. "There are times when he acts like . . . like he's got this great big secret."

"Aw, you're just imagining things."

Mary paused, wondering if perhaps her father was right. Then she said, "It's not my imagination that he's the most stubborn man I've ever seen."

Milt's eyes twinkled and his mouth curled into a teasing smile. "Most stubborn . . . or the least romantic?"

Mary felt her cheeks grow warm, and she busied herself at folding the blanket Livery had left on the counter. "Don't be ridiculous," she huffed, and wondered why her father's teasing made her feel suddenly embarrassed.

Ward paced back and forth in the small storeroom, angry with himself for letting Mary's questions bring him dangerously close to saying more than he wanted to about his past. In spite of how good these people had been to him, he didn't want them—or anyone else for that matter—knowing who or what he was, certainly not until he could handle a gun again.

He went to the bottom drawer of the bureau and

took out a cloth-wrapped package he had found among the odds and ends of clothes. He laid it on the bed and unwrapped it. The silver conch gleamed on the black holster that encased the lethal beauty of a silver, ivory-handled .45 Colt revolver. As he had every day for the past week, Ward gingerly eased his arm out of the sling and strapped on the gun belt, being careful not to move too quickly. He rubbed his wounded shoulder. It was stiff and still very sore.

Then he let his fingers close around the butt of the six-shooter. It felt good to his touch, like shaking hands with an old friend. Though he meant to draw the weapon slowly, instinct and years of habit took over, and he whipped the .45 out of the holster without conscious thought. Pain seared his shoulder and he was barely able to clear leather before he had to drop his arm to his side, the six-shooter hanging uselessly in his hand. He stood that way for what seemed like several minutes before the pain subsided. Then, as he eased the .45 back into the holster and undid the gun belt, he told himself he would have to play storekeeper for a while longer—maybe for a long while.

Royce tied up his mount at the hitch rail outside the cantina. The village square was practically deserted. It was siesta time. A few lazy flies buzzed in chorus and their green bodies glinted in the sunlight. His horse slapped at them with its tail while the flesh quivered over its rump. Royce dismounted and watched as two old and bent *peones* urged their floppy-eared burros through the dust of the sunbaked street, past a vaquero dozing in an open doorway, his face concealed under his broad sombrero. Except for the quiet and the absence of people, the grubby little town seemed about the same as it was the last time Royce had seen it—the day he had stood in this same spot watching the cock fight. The day he'd killed the man named Ward.

Though Archer claimed Ward wasn't dead, Royce knew otherwise. In his mind's eye he could see the young cowboy lying on his back in the street, spread-eagle, his six-shooter still in that fancy holster he wore. But then again, Royce hadn't actually checked to make sure he was dead. He shrugged and chuckled to himself. *Who cares?* he thought. If Archer was willing to pay him again to kill a man who was already dead, that was his business. He took a gold-plated watch out of a shirt pocket and checked the time. He had an hour before Archer was due to show up, so he headed for the cantina.

Ward stood at the only window in the storeroom and looked out as the gathering darkness draped what he could see of the town in deep shadow. Across the street, a single lantern cast a feeble glow on the open entrance to the blacksmith shop where the dying embers of the forge winked their red eyes in the early night.

He rubbed his wounded shoulder while he worked the fingers of his right hand, rhythmically opening and clenching his fist. As night filled the storeroom, a gloom descended over him like a weight. Somewhere out there was the man who had killed his brother. *Why did it have to be him?* he asked himself. *He'd been a man that was all good. If anyone had to die, it should have been me.* As his melancholy deepened, he began to wonder if the man who killed his brother could have been one of the same men that tried to kill him. That wasn't likely, he decided. Those men had probably just been ten-dollar-a-month cowpokes trying to steal a few beeves from their boss's herd. It was just plain bad luck that they had spotted Ward watching them that day.

He suddenly felt the need to get out of the tiny room, to be somewhere he could stop thinking about how long it would be before he was fast enough with a gun again to make it safe to get back on the trail of his brother's killer. He let himself out the door that opened onto the alley, being careful not to make any noise that could be heard by the Wells family in their living quarters on the floor above. He was willing to accept their kindness and charity for the moment because there was nothing else he could do, but he was starting to feel like he was in prison—a gentle one perhaps, but still a prison.

As he rounded the corner onto the main street, he could hear the quiet tinkle of a piano and the sound of voices drifting out of the Red Dog Saloon directly across from the general store. The lantern light that shone through the slats in the swinging doors was a cheery beacon in the otherwise-dark town.

Halfway across the street he had a strange sensation that he was being watched. He paused and looked back toward the store. Mary Wells was framed in the lighted window above the front door. Had she been watching him all along, or had she just happened to look out? He wasn't sure, but he knew she had seen him and knew she wouldn't like where he was headed. *Too bad,* he thought, and continued across the street.

As he reached the steps leading up to the saloon, the doors swung open and a beautiful, statuesque woman swished out onto the board sidewalk, her green taffeta dress rippling and swirling around her slippered feet. When she saw Ward she stopped, her coppery hair back-lit by the soft glow from the saloon. Their eyes met and she held his gaze, appraising him openly and with some obvious enjoyment. Her full red lips moved in just a hint of a smile before she continued down the sidewalk into the night that was lit now by a sliver of moon. Ward continued to watch her as she walked past the jail, and for the first time he noticed a mounted man in the shadows, just sitting astride his horse and watching. "Good evening, Sheriff," the woman said, as she strolled by. The sheriff touched a hand to his Stetson but didn't speak, and after she passed, he turned his gaze on Ward. Even in the weak light, Ward could tell it wasn't a friendly look.

He paused at the saloon entrance and glanced back again at the general store. Mary was still watching, her face troubled. When she saw him looking up at her, she stepped quickly away from the window and the room behind her went dark. *Must be a good night for watching,* Ward thought, glancing at the sheriff again before he pushed through the swinging doors.

The saloon was quiet. The piano player accompanied himself as he sang a sentimental tune. A couple of middle-aged women sat at a corner table talking and laughing with a dusty cowboy while he poured whiskey for them from his bottle. At the bar, a chubby man with a ruddy, cheerful-looking face, a glass of whiskey in front of him, stood talking with the bartender. He turned as Ward approached the bar.

"A good evenin' to you, me boy." He stuck out his hand. "I've wondered when I'd see you up and around. The name's Hennessey—Matthew Hennessey. Most folks call me Matt."

Ward knew he had seen this man before. Then it

came to him where. He was about to say something about the day that Hennessey had helped him up out of the street but thought better of it. There was no need to mention that he could recall the incident. "Good evening," he said, shaking the man's hand. "My name's Livery."

"We've already met." Matt smiled. "But you wasn't in the best of shape that day, so you might not remember. Will you join me in a drink, lad?"

Ward nodded. "Don't mind if I do." Hennessey signaled to the bartender and while he waited for his drink Ward said, "By the way, I passed a woman on the way in here—tall, with red hair, and she looked like real class. Know who she was?"

"You'd be meanin' Priscilla," Matt replied, "Priscilla Scanlon." He raised his glass in a salute. "Now she's a fine Irish lass if ever there was one."

"You wouldn't expect to see a woman like her in a . . ." Ward paused and looked around the room. "Does she come in here often?"

"You could say that," Hennessey replied. "She owns the place."

Chapter Six

It was growing dark when Clay Archer rode into the small Mexican village. The heat of the day had begun to ease, but he was still looking forward to having a beer after spending most of the day in the saddle. What he wasn't looking forward to was another meeting with Royce. He didn't like the man; he didn't even trust him. But worst of all he was afraid of him. It was something about his eyes; they were dark and cruel, constantly filled with menace. And it bothered him that Royce had demanded that they meet here, in this dusty border town. This was where he claimed he had killed Ward, and according to the note the old stage driver had delivered to Archer, Royce had some important news. *It's about time,* Archer thought. He had already promised to pay him—a second time—to find Ward and kill him. That had been nearly a month ago and this was the first he had heard from him since then.

As Archer rode by the shops and open stalls, peasants eyed him curiously from in front of their doorways that were bathed in the soft glow of the lanterns hanging in-side, already lit in anticipation of the coming night. But the brightest light was coming from the cantina halfway down the street. It was where Royce had said he wanted to meet. As Archer drew near, the quiet of the early eve-ning was shattered by a scream and then a gunshot. He reined up just as the cantina doors flew open and a young vaquero stumbled out onto the street. He had a six-shooter strapped to his hip, and was holding one arm with a hand that was awash with blood. He took a few staggering steps, then stood weaving like a reed in a stiff breeze, and wide-eyed shopkeepers moved off the street and into their shops.

The cantina doors swung open again and Royce swaggered out onto the steps. A few eager men, their faces a mixture of fear and curiosity, jammed the door-way behind him, while the remaining peasants along the street scurried into their homes. Royce stood spread legged, his hands on his hips. Archer thought he looked like a creature from hell, dressed all in black and out-lined against the devilish glow of the lantern light be-hind him.

"I told you what would happen if you got in my way again," he snarled at the wounded man.

The young vaguero glared at Royce, his dark eyes filled with hatred. He trembled with rage, then screamed, "Murderer!"

Royce laughed without humor, his lips curled in more of a sneer than a smile.

"Murderer!" the vaquero yelled again in a voice hoarse with emotion.

"Draw!" Royce commanded, and held his hand over his Colt. "Draw or I'll kill you where you stand." Even in the weak light, Archer could see the cruel, evil glint in his eyes, and the hint of pleasure around the thin lips that had twisted into a perverted smile. He shivered.

The young Mexican made a desperate, pathetic grasp for his gun. With one fluid motion, Royce drew and fired and the vaquero was slammed back against a hitch rail by the force of the .45 slug—dead before his six-shooter had ever left its holster. As the young man slid to the ground, Royce turned and sauntered back into the cantina. A few peasants ventured cautiously into the street and went to the dead man's side. They paid no attention to Archer as he dismounted, tied up his horse, and made his way up the cantina steps.

Inside he found Royce at a table, a bottle of tequila and a glass in front of him. Archer pulled out a chair and sat down. "You find Ward yet?" he asked in a voice that trembled slightly.

Royce took a folded piece of paper out of his pocket and passed it across the table.

Archer opened it and spread it in front of him, smoothing out the creases. On it was a sketch of Ward, with printing under it, and though the words were in Spanish, Archer suspected that it might be some kind of a wanted poster. "I don't read Mex," he said, and pushed the paper back in Royce's direction.

"Ward was in jail down here for murder," Royce told him. "He broke out three months ago."

"Somethin's fishy here," Archer replied. "You say you killed him. How could he have been in jail?"

Royce laughed. "You tell me."

He poured another shot of tequila and pushed the bottle toward Archer and motioned to an empty glass. Archer shook his head. "Someone must know what happened to him."

Royce pointed to the front door. "Someone did. But he didn't want to tell me."

"You mean . . . the man in the street?"

Royce nodded, and downed his drink in one swallow.

"Then why'd you kill him?" Archer demanded, growing suddenly angry. "He sure ain't goin' to tell you now."

"I didn't like his attitude. He was cocky, a showoff, thought he could outdraw me. I gave him a chance to just let things slide, but he wanted to take it out in the street—a big mistake." Royce grinned and poured another glass of tequila. Archer wondered how someone who had just killed a man could sit drinking and talking as though nothing had happened. *But,* he told himself, *that's just the kind of man I need right now.*

Archer's voice was low and urgent when he spoke. "Find him, Royce," he said. "Find Ward and kill him."

"Look," Ward said, "you gave me a job and a place to stay, and I appreciate it. But I don't feel right about this—intruding on your family . . ."

"That's nonsense," Milt interrupted. "You can't go on taking your meals in the storeroom. It was one thing when you were laid up, but you're nearly fit now."

They were sitting at the table in the dining room of the Wells' living quarters above the general store. Milt had insisted that Ward join him and Mary for breakfast, and for all his meals from now on for however long he might be staying with them. He was grateful for the older man's kindness, but something bothered him about the prospects of such an arrangement. For one thing, Ward felt this was just not the kind of place for him, not with these good people. If he had been more like his brother, maybe things would be . . . He put the thought out of his mind. Besides, he didn't want to get too close to the Wells family, especially Mary. He could see where it might just be too easy to become attached to this pretty, bright woman, and Ward had no time for attachments right now. He had other things on his mind.

And Milt was right—he was almost fit. If only he could regain the speed with his gun hand. But that was another thought he didn't want to dwell on right now.

Yet the main reason he wanted to keep his distance was because he didn't want these people to know about his past; he came from a life they wouldn't understand, especially Mary. So until he was ready to move on, it was better to pretend he had lost his memory; it made answering their questions easier—by not answering them. "But what if I'm not the kind of man you want at your table?" Ward said, hoping to give Milt an easy excuse to withdraw his offer.

"I'll take that chance," he answered.

"So will I." Mary came in from the kitchen carrying a tray of fresh steaming biscuits and set it on the well-stocked table. She smiled at Ward and took a seat across from her father.

"As I said," Ward continued, "I'm grateful for all you've done taking care of me, the job in the store. But it's time . . ." He shrugged. He was beginning to feel like the situation was closing in on him. "It's time to move on."

"What's the hurry?" Mary asked, an edge of concern in her voice. She got up and began loading food on their plates.

"Wait a while," Milt urged. "Make sure you've got your strength back."

"But you don't know anything about me," Ward insisted. "I don't even know anything about myself," he added quickly. Mary stopped what she was doing and glanced at him. He thought she looked skeptical, maybe even suspicious, and he turned his eyes away from hers.

She gave them each a plate of food and returned to her seat. "What do you think you are, a vicious killer or something?"

Ward looked up sharply. Then he focused his attention on his napkin, unfolding it slowly and deliberately, trying to stay calm, but unable to shake the feeling that Mary was still staring at him. Avoiding her eyes, he reached for a biscuit, broke it open, and took a bite.

Milt cleared his throat softly, and Ward looked up in time to see Mary fold her hands and bow her head. He suddenly felt more out of place than ever. "This isn't for me," he growled, and pushed his chair back from the table.

"Give it a chance," Milt urged gently. "We don't expect miracles." There was an awkward silence for a moment as the older man's eyes pleaded. Mary stared into her food and toyed with the fork on her plate, the faint clinking the only sound in the room.

"I told you," Ward repeated, trying to keep the harshness out of his tone, "this isn't for me." He threw his napkin down on the table, stood up, and headed toward the doorway leading to the main floor. As he started down the stairs he heard Milt say, "He needs time—and patience." There was no response from Mary.

Later that morning, still feeling glum and increasingly doubtful as to whether he should remain in the Wells' employ, Ward nevertheless resumed his regular duties in the general store. As he wandered among the shelves and display cases taking inventory and making notes in the small ledger he carried, he was suddenly aware of another presence in the room. He glanced up to see Mary go quietly behind the main counter and begin to wield a feather duster with unusual ferocity. She avoided his look and her face was a stern mask, which only deepened the chill brought on by her lack of a customary greeting. Ward looked away, returning to his inventory. Then he glanced up quickly again to catch Mary watching him. They stared at each other for a moment, and then her pretty face brightened in a wide smile.

"This is so silly," she said, and put down the feather duster and began to rearrange the candy jars on the counter.

Ward felt a sense of relief he didn't quite understand. "I agree," he said and smiled in return.

Mary sobered, and her look became pensive. After a pause she said, "You know, I find it strange you can remember where practically everything in this store goes and how much it costs, but you can't remember where you're from . . . or what you did for a living."

"Maybe I was a storekeeper, after all."

Mary frowned, and her face darkened. "I wouldn't think that's very likely. You were . . . wearing a gun when we took you in."

Ward ignored her comment and concentrated on the ledger in his hand.

"Don't you remember?" she said after a pause. "You must remember. If you were a storekeeper, why were you wearing a gun?"

"Maybe I got robbed a lot," Ward said, and forced a laugh, hoping to change the subject.

Mary failed to see the humor in the remark. "Sometimes I think you don't want to remember," she said sharply, and resumed dusting the shelves furiously.

Ward watched her, not sure what to do or how to respond. She was coming dangerously close to the truth with her questioning. And although he knew it would involve considerable risk, he had a surprising urge to take her into his confidence, to tell her everything there was to know about himself and his past.

He walked to her and took the duster from her hand and laid it on the counter. Then he held her gently by the shoulders and looked deeply into her eyes. She uttered a small gasp as he drew her close. He stopped, as a small voice nagged at him. *Don't be a fool,* he told himself and gently pushed her away.

Mary looked perplexed; her brow wrinkled.

He turned his back to her, then walked to the window and stood staring out at the street.

"John," she said softly, "can't you just tell me . . . ?" Before she could finish, the front door opened and Priscilla Scanlon swept into the store, resplendent in a green silk dress with a matching broad-brimmed hat that complemented the coppery tresses that fell to her shoulders. She paused for a moment just inside the door as though sensing the tension that permeated the room. Then her piercing green eyes sought out Ward and, as she had the night in front of the saloon, she appraised him openly. He returned her stare, struck by the beauty of her face and form, even more striking now in the light of day.

Their exchange of looks was not lost on Mary, and Ward thought she appeared suddenly angry. "Is there something I can do for you, Miss Scanlon?" she said, her tone unusually cool.

"Oh, Mary, yes— did that dress material and my hats come in yet?"

"They're all ready for you." Mary reached behind the counter and produced two bolts of cloth and several hat-boxes of various sizes. It was clear she was annoyed as Priscilla and Ward continued to eye each other frankly. "That'll be thirty dollars," Mary snapped.

"Would you put it on my bill?" Priscilla said as she went to the counter. She began to collect her things but was unable to handle all the packages at once. "Oh, Mary, my buggy's just up the street. Do you suppose someone could . . . ?"

Ward was across the room before she could say another word. Mary glared at him. "I'm sure we could find somebody," she muttered icily, while he began to load the bolts of cloth and hatboxes into his arms.

Priscilla's eyes twinkled and, ignoring Mary's scowl, she smiled demurely as she picked up the remaining boxes and led him to the door.

Outside, with her head erect and her silk skirt rustling with each quick stride, Priscilla preceded Ward along the wooden sidewalk toward her carriage that was tied at the hitch rail farther up the street. Ward smiled to himself as he watched the envious glances of the few women they passed and the leers of the men. When they got to the carriage, he stacked the packages he was carrying in the storage area behind the seat, then turned to help Priscilla. As she handed him the last hatbox, their fingers touched and she let her hand linger on his for a moment. A faint smile played across her ruby lips then vanished.

"This is very kind of you, Mister . . . ?"

"My name is Livery—John Livery."

He went to the hitch rail and untied her horse and held it steady while Priscilla mounted her carriage. Again she gave him a long, penetrating look. "Thank you, Mr. Livery. One rarely meets a true gentleman these days," she said with a small, provocative smile, "especially one who is also so . . . attractive."

Ward returned her gaze. "It's my job," he said flatly.

"What a pity. I was hoping it might have been . . . something more."

Priscilla snapped the reins over the back of her horse and moved the rig out into the street, maneuvering it skillfully between several riders and an assortment of other buggies and wagons. Ward followed her with his eyes until she turned at the first corner, and as she drove out of sight he noticed a rider who had just reined up in front of the telegraph office. The man looked familiar, but Ward might not have recognized him had it not been for the star pinned to his vest.

Without looking either right or left, the sheriff walked briskly to the telegraph office and disappeared inside.

Ward turned back toward the general store. Mary was standing in the doorway, her arms folded and a pout on her face. When she saw him start in her direction, he was bemused to see that she ducked quickly inside and slammed the door behind her.

Chapter Seven

"So it's taking a little longer to find him than I thought," Royce said.

"It's takin' a *lot* longer than you thought," Archer replied. "You told me the same thing a week ago."

"It's not easy tracking a ghost."

They were in a wooded draw on the edge of the Kelso ranch. Archer had sent word to Royce that he needed to see him. Even though he was afraid of Royce he was tired of waiting to hear if he had finally killed Ward. They had both dismounted, and now they stood talking while their horses drank from the shallow stream that flowed through the draw.

"That trip to Mexico was a waste of time," Archer growled.

"It was your idea," Royce answered.

"No matter—I'm gettin' tired of waitin'."

Royce shrugged. "Then find him yourself."

"I just might, if it takes much longer. You got one more week or . . ."

"Or what?" Royce's eyes narrowed to slits.

"Or . . . or you can forget about bein' paid," Archer said meekly, trying to assert himself but not wanting to anger the gunfighter.

Royce laughed out loud but there was no humor in it. "You're a funny man," he said, "not very smart, but funny." He retrieved his horse and swung up into the saddle.

A mixture of nervousness and fear made Archer feel sick to his stomach. "How much longer is it goin' to take?" he asked, trying to hide the flutter in his voice.

"Oh, it won't take long at all," Royce replied, "that is, if he's really alive." He started slowly out of the draw. "I think I'll try looking a little closer to home," he added, just before he was lost from sight in the trees.

"I'm real glad you finally decided to join us for Sunday services, John." Milt Wells shrugged into a black frock coat and looked in the mirror over the dry goods counter while he adjusted his string tie. "I'm going on ahead," he announced as he started across the room. He paused at the door and said, "I'll see you two in church."

"I'm glad you're going too," Mary told John after Milt had left. "But I must say I'm surprised." There was a hint of criticism in her voice.

"I'm a little surprised, myself," he said while he

watched her secure her bonnet with a large bow under her chin. He didn't want to tell her that he had agreed to go to church in hopes that it might improve her disposition. It would be a lot more pleasant for everyone if she would get over her snit. She had been cold and grumpy ever since the day he had helped Priscilla Scanlon out to her carriage with her packages.

"We'd better go, then," Mary said, her tone still frosty. "We don't want to be late."

Outside, they walked in silence toward the small, white clapboard church on the edge of town, its cross-topped steeple gleaming in the morning sun, and joined the other townspeople making their way up the front steps. Inside, most of the rough wooden pews were already filled.

Matt Hennessey saw them and motioned to the space next to him on the crowded bench.

Ward looked around the small nave and felt self-conscious, strangely out of place. He could hardly remember the last time he had been inside a church. It had been with his father and brother, at his mother's funeral. "Where's your father?" he whispered to Mary after they were seated.

She nodded toward the front of the nave. A tall man in a black frock coat, his back to the congregation, was arranging some papers at the small pulpit. Just as Ward looked up, the man turned around. It was Milt.

"Why didn't you tell me?" he whispered.

"Why—would it have made any difference?"

"No—well, maybe it would have." Ward hesitated. "I don't know. It's just that you . . . you could have told me—after all this time."

"Shhh—services are going to start."

I guess now I understand why he takes in people like me, Ward thought as Milt began to speak. And though he felt a deep and growing gratitude for the man at the pulpit, he also felt a jolting awareness of just how truly different they were. *This man is all good,* he mused, *and I'm . . . well, I am who I am.* He forced the thought out of his mind, and as he leaned back to listen to Milt, he resolved to separate himself from the lives of the Wells family as soon as possible. But he couldn't explain the strange gloom that settled over him at the idea of it.

Later, as the service ended, Ward was still feeling sullen. He followed Mary Wells and Matt Hennessey out the front door to where Milt waited on the top step, shaking hands with the departing worshippers.

"Well, John," he said with a broad smile, "that wasn't too painful now, was it?" He held out his hand. "What'd you think?"

"I think life is full of surprises," Ward replied without enthusiasm and returned Milt's handshake. They stood for a moment without either man speaking.

"That was a good sermon, Milt," Hennessey chimed in finally, breaking the silence.

Milt gazed at Ward, a faint, almost sad, smile on his lips. "I'm not sure everyone shares your opinion, Matt."

Ward shrugged and started down the church steps followed closely by Mary and Hennessey. The threesome made their way back toward the center of town in silence, with Ward deep in thought about what would be the best way to end his relationship with Mary and her father.

"Milt sure had some good things to say today, John," Matt said, his eyes twinkling and a lilt in his brogue, obviously trying to penetrate the gloom. "As a matter of fact, it seemed like he almost had you in mind."

Ward gave him a questioning look but said nothing.

"For instance, there was what he said about how we all have to choose the path we're goin' to follow in life," Matt went on, "and about gettin' a new start."

"It's hard to choose a new path when you don't remember the old one." Ward's tone was gruff.

Mary gave him a skeptical look. "I disagree," she said, before hesitating as though deep in thought. Then her face brightened in a faint smile. "It seems to me you've got the chance of a lifetime—no past . . . all future. You can take any direction you want." Then she added softly, "It can even be one that doesn't involve a gun."

Ward bristled. "Men carry guns for different reasons," he growled.

"And none of those reasons are good," Mary replied sharply. "What was yours? Oh, yes, forgive me. You don't remember."

Again Ward had to fight the impulse to answer Mary's challenge—and to risk exposing information he wanted kept secret. He shoved his hands deep into his pockets and walked along in silence as his sense of gloom deepened.

Mary and Hennessey exchanged an embarrassed glance but neither spoke.

Then the awkward stillness was broken by the clomp of a horse's hooves and the crunch of wheels in the sandy street. They all looked up as Priscilla Scanlon, sitting erect and looking queenly, rode by in her buggy. She was dressed in an elegant high-collar dress, and a pert flowered hat topped her flaming tresses. She smiled and nodded to the group, but it was obvious that her eyes were for Ward. He returned her gaze and held it until she turned her attention back to her driving.

The exchange wasn't lost on Mary, and the scowl that crossed her face turned the sunny day dark; she quickened her pace toward the center of town, leaving Ward and Hennessey struggling to keep up.

"Ah . . . if you two'll excuse me," Hennessey huffed as they approached his restaurant, "I got to get ready for the Sunday crowd. I'll see you later." He veered off and left Mary and Ward striding along in silence.

"Hey, you two, wait up!" They both turned to see Milt striding up from behind. "What's the rush?" he asked when he caught up to them. "Today's Sunday," he said, puffing. "It's supposed to be a day of rest. You two act like you're going to a fire." Neither Mary nor Ward responded. "What's for dinner, Mary?" Milt said after a moment, forcing a smile. He glanced quickly from his daughter to Ward and his smile faded.

"We're having fried chicken," Mary replied glumly as they neared the general store.

"Mmm, that's my favorite," Milt said with an exaggerated smack of his lips. "How about you, John—you think fried chicken sounds good?"

"Thanks just the same. I think I better start taking my meals at Hennessey's from now on." He broke off from the group and started toward the Irishman's restaurant.

"Wait," Milt said, "there's no need to do that."

Ward ignored his entreaty.

"Oh, let him go," Mary said loud enough for Ward to hear, and stomped up the steps and into the store without looking back.

When Ward got to the restaurant he was glad to find that it was empty; he wasn't in the mood for seeing people. Hennessey was behind the counter stacking plates and arranging silverware. He looked up when

Ward came in, and his thick eyebrows raised in an unasked question. He tied a slightly soiled apron high around his waist and motioned to one of the vacant tables that filled the room. "Have a seat," he said.

"Not now—I just came in to look the place over." Ward went to an easel propped up on one end of the counter and stood reading the menu items that were written on a slate.

"How 'bout a nice bowl of me Irish stew?" Hennessey urged. "I'll vow it's the best in the state—maybe in the country."

Ward shook his head and started toward the door. Hennessey followed him out onto the wooden sidewalk. "You're makin' a big mistake, me boy, not tryin' some of me stew."

"There'll be other chances," Ward said. "Starting tomorrow I'll be having all my meals here . . . until I leave town."

"Oh?" Hennessey said. He stopped Ward with an arm on his shoulder and stood for a moment, a thoughtful look on his face. "Are you sure that's wise?"

"I've imposed on the Wells family long enough."

"That's your business, of course," Hennessey said after another long pause, "but I've heard Mary's a mighty fine cook." He leaned closer to Ward and looked around quickly as though afraid he'd be overheard. "I wouldn't want this to get around, mind you," he added, in a conspiratorial tone, "but her cookin' might even be better than mine."

Ward grinned at the Irishman's confession.

"And I've heard . . . well, some say she's even a mite sweet on you."

Ward's smile faded. He knew that Hennessey was probably right, but hearing someone say it out loud still came as a surprise, somehow a disturbing one. "Yeah," he said quietly and stepped down off the sidewalk. "Anyway, I'll be gone soon. I just need to . . . well, there's something I need to do to get ready, and then I'm gone." He told himself it shouldn't be long before he regained his quickness with a gun. "So it doesn't really matter," Ward added.

Hennessey paused for a moment with a perplexed look on his face, mumbling to himself, then went back into his restaurant.

Ward started across the street toward the saloon.

He had only taken a few steps when a harsh voice rang out. "Ward!"

He spun in his tracks, crouching. Instinctively, his hand went to his hip for the gun that wasn't there. He stood feeling naked and helpless, and stared into the stern face of Sheriff Travis Dutton.

Chapter Eight

"**S**o now that you know who I am, what do you intend to do about it?" Ward was standing with his back to Dutton and thumbing through a stack of wanted posters that hung on the wall in the sheriff's office.

"Nothing . . . for the moment," the sheriff said from behind his desk. "In the first place, I don't have any jurisdiction over Mexican jailbirds—even convicted killers. Second, you won't be around that long."

Ward turned to face him. "Oh, no?"

"Take my word for it. This is a quiet town. We don't cotton to escaped convicts . . . from either side of the border."

Ward gave him a hard look, then went back to thumbing through the posters. "So, are there any pictures of me in here?"

"You'd've been the first to know if there had been."

"Then how'd you find out . . . ?"

"The Federal marshal helped. It took a long time to

79

get a line on you. I telegraphed him right after you got to town."

"Why would you do that," Ward asked him, "if there was no paper on me?"

Dutton chuckled. "A stranger gets dumped off the stage, all shot up, wearin' a gun," he said cynically. "What would you do if you was in my shoes?"

Ward shrugged, silently conceding he would have probably done the same thing.

"I was plannin' to come over to the general store to check on you," Dutton continued, "but decided to wait since I didn't see your picture in that batch." He pointed to the posters Ward had been looking through. "Then the marshal finally sent me these." He pulled a small sheaf of papers out of a drawer and tossed them on the desk. "It just so happened they had a couple of Mexican ones mixed in."

Ward shuffled through them until he came to one with a sketch of his face on it. The printing was in Spanish, but it didn't matter because he was sure he knew what it said. He flipped through the rest of the posters without interest until another one in Spanish caught his eye. Even in the sketch, the man on the poster had evil, penetrating eyes, and wore a cruel grin on his face. His hat and shirt were penciled black. Ward recognized the same Spanish words that were on his own poster. Whoever this man was, he too was wanted in Mexico for murder.

He handed the flyers back to Dutton. "Does anyone else have to know about me? I'd just as soon stay John Livery for the time being."

"It's none of my business what name a man uses . . . long as he's just passin' through town."

Ward was a little surprised that the sheriff agreed so readily to keep silent. But he didn't want to give him a chance to change his mind, so he grunted a quick, "Thanks," and started for the door.

"And Ward . . ." Dutton said, the sudden menace in his tone making Ward stop and turn. "Believe me when I say you *are* just passin' through—so don't be too slow about leavin'."

Ward went out of the sheriff's office and strode quickly across the street toward the general store. He chose not to use the front entrance, but instead went down the alley at the side of the building and let himself in through the door that opened into the storeroom that served as his living quarters. He went straight to the old bureau and took his gun and holster, still wrapped in a cloth, out of the drawer. He unwrapped it and slipped the six-shooter out of its holster. There was a soft whirring sound as he spun the cylinder, and then he loaded it with cartridges and eased the weapon back into the holster and rewrapped it in the cloth.

With his bundle under one arm, he went to the door across the room and walked into the main area of the general store.

Milt was stacking five-pound bags of flour in front of the counter while Mary made notations in a ledger. They both looked up when he came in. "John," Milt said cheerily, "did you decide to have dinner with us after all? We'll be eating in about an hour."

Mary put down the ledger and eyed the bundle under his arm. Her face grew dark, but she didn't speak.

"No, thanks," Ward said. "I just came in to ask you a favor."

"Name it," Milt replied.

"Could I borrow a horse?"

Milt smiled and gave Mary a glance that seemed to say *I told you so.* "Oh, I forgot to mention it," he said, smiling at Ward. "The stagecoach driver found a horse wandering near where he picked you up—brought him in just yesterday morning."

"Oh?" Ward said cautiously.

"He left him at the livery stable," Milt went on. "It could be he's yours."

"Thanks," Ward said in a noncommittal tone, "that could be, I suppose." He nodded to Milt, and without looking at Mary, crossed to the front door and went out. He paused for a minute on the wooden sidewalk, trying to decide how to claim the horse, if indeed it was his, without revealing that his memory had returned.

"See," he heard Milt say quietly, "I told you. He didn't remember he even had a horse."

"He didn't remember," Mary answered, "or he just figured it was gone for good, so why mention it?"

Smart girl, Ward said to himself as he stepped down off the sidewalk and started for the livery stable. He found the attendant pitching hay into a stall where a beautiful roan chomped on it eagerly. As Ward approached, the horse stopped eating and looked up, ears erect and nostrils flaring as he sniffed noisily.

"Howdy," the man said, "what can I do for ya?"

"I heard the stage driver found a horse out on the trail. Is this it?"

The man nodded and squinted, a cautious look on his face. "You lose a horse?"

Ward shrugged.

"You think he might be yours?"

"My memory's been a little shaky lately," Ward told him. "He could be." The roan whinnied eagerly and pressed against the stall door while he pawed the floor.

"Way he's actin'," the man said, suddenly smiling, "I'd almost bet on it."

"Then I'll take him off your hands."

"Give me four bits for a day's rent and feed, and he's yours," the man said. "Your saddle and all's right there." He pointed to the tack hanging on a wall between the stalls.

The roan nickered contentedly while Ward put on his saddle and halter and stowed his wrapped-up revolver in the saddlebag. He paid the man and rode out of the stable, enjoying the familiar feel of his mount under him and relishing the pleasure that came from being re-united with an old friend. He headed out of town and rode for about a half hour until he came to a secluded area on the edge of a dry streambed hidden by cotton-woods and mesquites.

He dismounted, secured his horse, and took his six-shooter out of his saddlebag and strapped it on. Then he gathered up several fist-sized rocks and set them side by side about six inches apart on the trunk of a fallen mesquite. When he had them arranged the way he wanted, he paced off about thirty feet and turned and faced the rocks. He held his hand over his weapon, flex-ing his fingers, and then, with all the quickness he could muster, he drew and fired four times in rapid suc-cession. With the explosion of sound, splinters flew off the rotted trunk, but when the smoke had cleared all but one of the rocks were still there, silently mocking his marksmanship. He winced at the pain that lingered in his shoulder, but his real agony was reserved for the pathetic slowness of his draw and his lack of accuracy.

Slowly he reloaded his gun and dropped it back in the holster. Then, his mind focused on the task at hand, he drew and fired several more shots. Except for some-what less pain and his feeling that perhaps his draw had been a fraction of a second faster, the results were about the same: flying chips of wood but no rocks. But his determination was firm. So for about the next half hour he repeated the process over and over until his aching shoulder, depleted ammunition, and approaching darkness decreed that he had had enough for the first of what would be many painful days on the road that would ultimately lead to his brother's killer.

Matt Hennessey came out of his restaurant and locked the door behind him. The dinner crowd had been sparse and, though it wasn't quite dark, with the customers all gone he saw no point in staying open. As he stepped into the deserted street he saw a rider approaching. In the fading light it took Matt a few seconds to make out that it was John Livery.

"John, me boy!" he called out and waved. "It's not too late for a bowl of me stew. I could warm some up in the wink of an eye."

Livery dismounted and tied up his horse at the hitch rail in front of the general store.

As Hennessey walked in his direction, he noticed for the first time that Livery was wearing a gun. He unbuckled it, wrapped it in some kind of a cloth, and put it in his saddlebag.

"Anything wrong, lad?" Hennessey said, when he was close enough to see the gloomy scowl on the other man's face. "You look like you lost somethin' near and dear."

"I have," Livery said quietly. He stood for a moment with downcast eyes and his hand resting on the saddlebag. "And I'm not sure I'll ever get it back."

"What was it, lad?"

"Forget it."

Matt put an arm on his shoulder. "What you need is somethin' to cheer you up."

"No stew—I don't want any stew," Livery replied quickly.

Hennessey laughed. "No, no," he said, "but I'll see that you get the next best thing." He pointed to the saloon across the street with the light already spilling out of its front door. "Come on over to the Red Dog and I'll treat you to a drop of nectar straight from Ireland."

Livery shrugged. "Why not?"

"Why not, indeed," Hennessey said with a smile and led the way across the street. The crowd at the Red Dog was thin, with only a couple of guys Hennessey identified as regulars sitting at the bar and a few scruffy cowboys scattered among the tables. At the bar, Hennessey motioned to a pudgy man who stood a few feet off, twirling one end of his handlebar moustache and seemingly lost in another world.

"Barkeep!" Matt's voice snapped the man awake.

"What'll it be?" he said sullenly as he walked toward the pair at the bar.

"We'll take two glasses of heavenly dew from the old sod." Hennessey's tone caressed the words.

"We ain't got none of that," the barman said.

"He means Irish whiskey," a husky female voice said.

The two men turned to see Priscilla Scanlon, wearing an elegant low-cut gown, gliding in their direction.

"I'll handle it," she said to the man with the moustache and went behind the bar. She placed an ornate, amber-colored bottle and two glasses in front of them and stared boldly at Livery, her green eyes flashing. "You seem surprised," she said as he regarded her with cool curiosity; but he said nothing as she poured whiskey in their glasses nearly up to the brim.

"You're uncommonly generous today, Priscilla darlin'," Hennessey said, and picked up his glass. "Would it be on account of me guest here?"

She smiled provocatively. "Maybe I'm just in a generous mood."

Hennessey took a healthy swallow, then closed his eyes and sighed.

Livery sipped his whiskey and nodded his approval, then raised his glass to Priscilla. "Here's to a thing of beauty."

"Aye," Matt agreed, "I'll drink to that."

"The whiskey's not bad either," Livery said as he and Priscilla flirted with their eyes.

Matt finished his drink and slapped some money on the bar. "How 'bout one more, lad?"

Livery finished his drink and shook his head. He stepped back from the bar, his eyes still on Priscilla. "Pleasure should be taken in moderation."

She smiled demurely. "I'll try to remember that. I'm used to getting what I want."

Livery gave her a lingering look, then nodded his thanks to Hennessey and headed for the door.

Mary stood in her darkened room over the general store and looked out the window as Livery came out of the saloon, retrieved his horse, and led it to the stable. Quietly, so as not to arouse her father, she slipped downstairs and let herself into the storeroom. Everything was bathed in pale moonlight that flooded in through the lone window and gave the room an almost ghostly glow. She stood in the shadows and waited.

In a few minutes, the door from the alley opened and Livery was framed in the faint light, the cloth-wrapped weapon in his hand. He crossed to the bureau where he pulled open a drawer and deposited his package.

"So, is that one of the things you didn't forget?" Mary said and stepped out of the shadows.

He spun to face her, and his surprised look turned to one of puzzlement.

"The gun," she added, "you remembered your gun?"

He eased the drawer closed and stood with his back to it. "How do you know it's a gun?"

"I took care of your things, remember?"

He went to the lamp next to his bunk and struck a match.

"No, don't light it." Mary's tone was pleading, urgent. "Please don't light it."

Livery blew out the flame.

"It's . . . it's easier to talk in the dark," she explained, and quickly moved closer to him and stood staring intently into his face. "Who are you?" she whispered after a short silence.

"You know who I am."

"All right, then, *what* are you? You're certainly not a storekeeper." She paused again. "You didn't really lose your memory, did you?"

"Why? What's the difference?"

"I've got to know." Mary moved a step closer and touched a hand to his face. Her heart thumped and her breath came quick and shallow. "I can't stand being near you like this and . . . and not knowing. What are you hiding?"

Livery grabbed her roughly by the shoulders and drew her close. Mary gasped, afraid her pounding heart would burst from her breast. She was frightened and repelled by this man, but at the same time was power-fully attracted to him. "You don't want to know," he said gruffly. "Leave it alone."

"I can't," Mary said, her voice trembling.

He leaned toward her, as though to kiss her, but then he thrust her away and held her at arm's length. His fingers dug into her shoulders. "You don't want anything to do with me."

"Let me decide that," Mary said as her breathing slowed.

His hands fell to his sides; his shoulders slumped. "You're right. I didn't lose my memory. I'm a wanted man. It was easier to pretend to be someone else than to have to answer people's questions." He turned away from her, toward the small window, and stood looking out at the night. When he turned back again he said, "Now do you understand?"

"No." Mary fought back the urge to go to him. "All I know is . . ."

She was interrupted by a soft knocking on the door that led to the street. Livery glanced around in surprise and moved quickly to answer it. Priscilla Scanlon, a cape drawn close about her neck and a hood covering her red hair, was silhouetted in the doorway. She smiled at him and stepped silently into the dim room. Then she saw Mary. Priscilla's smile faded, and she and Livery eyed each other awkwardly for a moment.

"I'm so sorry," Priscilla said. "I had no idea. . . . Please forgive me." She wheeled and started for the door.

"Wait." He stopped her with a hand on her arm. "Maybe now's not the time, but I need to talk to you. Could we meet sometime?"

Priscilla glanced at Mary then back to Livery. "You're sure?" He nodded. "Well, I'll be gone for a few days," Priscilla said, "but as soon as I return we can . . ."

"That's fine," he said quickly, and guided her to the door.

She paused and gave him a long thoughtful look, then, with another quick glance at Mary, slipped into the darkened street.

Livery turned. "Mary, I . . . it's not what you think."

Mary choked back a sob as she pushed past him and lunged through the open door, grateful for the night that hid her tears

Chapter Nine

Shortly before noon, Mary crossed the street to the livery stable and asked the man there to hitch up her father's buckboard.

"Got some deliveries to make?" he asked while he made a final adjustment to the harness.

"No," Mary replied, as she let the man help her up into the seat of the small rig, "just an errand to run." She clucked the horse into motion, then headed out into the street and out of town. She proceeded at a slow trot for about fifteen minutes, then turned off the main road onto a poorly defined trail that led toward a large stand of mesquites and ironwoods.

After a few more minutes she reined up and, at the edge of the tree line, climbed down from the wagon and hobbled her horse. The animal nickered softly and pricked up his ears at a sudden noise. Mary paused to listen. There was no mistaking the slow steady sound of gunfire coming from somewhere deep within the trees ahead. "It's all right, boy," she whispered reassuringly and stroked her horse's long face. "You wait here. I'll be back in a few minutes." Then she slipped among the trees, following the sound of the gunshots.

The noise grew louder as she picked her way through the thin forest, and she soon came to the edge of a well-concealed clearing. She stopped and watched as Livery, his back to her, blazed away with his six-shooter. Rocks, set in a row along a rotting fallen tree trunk, flew into the air in rapid succession until he emptied his weapon. Then he paused to reload and dropped his gun into its holster and, looking like a coiled spring, crouched with his hand poised over his hip—ready to draw again.

Mary stepped gingerly into the clearing, cautiously picking her way, but a dry twig snapped under her foot. Livery spun and whipped his Colt out of its holster in one fluid, lightening-fast motion. Mary sucked in a huge breath, terrified at the sight of the lethal weapon pointed straight at her heart, a heart that now raced so fast and beat so loud that the sound of it filled her ears.

Livery's eyes bulged, showing a mixture of fear and anger. Then his shoulders slumped and he lowered the gun to his side. As he gazed into Mary's eyes, the fear and anger turned to pain. "I could have killed you," he said in a soft voice that betrayed his agony.

Mary realized she was holding her breath and let out a long sigh. She began to tremble. Livery holstered his gun and went to her and wrapped her protectively in his arms as if to still her shaking. "Don't ever do anything like that again," he said, in a voice now edged with a kindly gruffness.

"I know. It . . . it was stupid of me."

"Seems a man can't have any secrets around here," he said, his tone stern. He held her at arm's length and his face darkened in a scowl. "How did you know where to find me?"

"Hennessey told me. He said he heard that you come out here just about every day."

"I don't like being followed."

"I'm sorry," Mary whispered. "But I had to see you . . . about last night." She looked up into his face, trying to penetrate the depths of the chips of blue ice that stared back at her. "John . . ."

He put a finger to her lips and shook his head as tears began to well up in Mary's eyes. "As soon as I can," he said firmly, "I'm leaving."

"Why can't you stay?"

"I'm looking for a man."

"Is he that important?"

"He is to me. He killed my brother." His look grew darker and he added, "He killed the only brother I had."

Mary shuddered. "And when you find this man," she said, "what then?" although she knew full well what his answer would be. Livery stared at her in silence. She stiffened her back and vowed to herself not to let him see her cry. "Do me one favor," she said after a moment, her voice even and firm, "please—before you make up your mind?"

"It's already made up."

"Just talk to my father. He's at the church."

"I told you, that stuff's not for me."

"It's not what you think." Mary put a hand on his arm. "What can it hurt to talk?"

After another long silence, Livery said, "I can't make any promises." Then, taking her by the elbow, he steered her back through the trees in the direction she had come from. "Come on, I'll take you back to your horse."

"It appears as though you've already decided what you're going to do," Milt said. "Why come to me now?"

He and Ward were standing on the steps of the church, in front of the open door. "It wasn't my idea," Ward said. "I did it as a favor to . . . to someone."

"Someone who's falling in love with you?" Milt smiled knowingly and nodded his head.

The question caught Ward by surprise. "Who said anything . . . ?" He felt the warmth rise in his cheeks. "You think you know who it was?"

"Unless I miss my guess, it was Mary," Milt answered. "We both know she's been taken with you almost since the day you came to town. But what you might not know is how much she's against guns and violence . . . senseless killing." He glanced at the six-shooter on Ward's hip.

"She's made that quite clear more than once."

"Then you had to know she'd want you to come here . . . to the church . . . sooner or later." He put a gentle hand on Ward's shoulder. "Look, John, you seem determined to hunt down this man, whoever he is, so I'm not going to preach to you. But just wait here a minute and let me show you something."

Ward watched as Milt went into the empty church and walked to the front of the nave and reached behind the small pulpit. He withdrew a holstered Colt .45 wrapped in its own cartridge belt. Ward was speechless when Milt returned and held out the weapon for him to see. "I keep this as a reminder."

"A reminder," Ward said after he found his voice. "Of what?"

Milt started down the church steps. "Let's go around back." Ward followed him and when they reached the grassy area behind the building Milt said, "There should be an old tin can or two around here somewhere from the last picnic. See if you can find one while I put this thing on." He stripped off his frock coat and strapped on the gun belt, and tied down the holster with a leather thong around his thigh.

"I still don't believe this," Ward said after he picked up a rusting can.

"Just toss it in the air," Milt told him, "anytime you're ready."

Ward threw the can high in the air, where it tumbled end over end. From a slight crouch, Milt drew with blazing speed and, fanning the hammer of his revolver, fired six shots from the hip in rapid succession, each one finding its mark and keeping the can bouncing crazily in the air as if being held up by an invisible hand. When the hammer of the Colt finally clicked on a spent shell, Milt straightened up and dropped the gun back into its holster.

Ward shook his head slowly. "I've seen some fast men," he said admiringly, "but you're about as good as they come."

Milt responded to the words of praise with a sad look, then undid the gun belt and wrapped it around the holster. "I'm good enough to have killed three men before I hung it up," he said, in a voice that sounded tired. "I've always regretted those killings . . . having to live with the memories." He paused and eyed the gun in his hands as though it were an object of contempt. "That's why I keep this thing. I never want to forget how wrong it was . . . how wrong I was."

"You must have had some good reasons," Ward said, feeling the remorse in the older man's words.

" 'Thou shalt not kill,' " Milt said quietly, his eyes glistening. "There are no good reasons, no excuses, no exceptions."

"Don't I remember something about 'an eye for an eye'?" Ward said, feeling suddenly defensive as he thought about his quest to avenge his brother.

Milt nodded. "Yes, and I've known men who used that as a justification for killing. But you might want to remember something else. 'Vengeance is mine, saith the Lord.' " He went to Ward, put a hand on his shoulder, and looked deep into his eyes. "It's your choice," he said quietly. "I told you I wouldn't preach." Then he turned and walked slowly back toward the front of the church.

Chapter Ten

"It took grit for you to meet me like this," Ward said to Priscilla Scanlon, "a strange man . . . all alone.

Pricilla smiled demurely. She was mounted sidesaddle on a handsome brown Tennessee Walker and Ward rode at her side on his roan. The horses moved at a leisurely walk along a trail cut through the gently sloping foothills of the Dragoon Mountains, their cylindrical spires shimmering in the hazy distance. "I didn't really think I had anything to fear," Priscilla said, with a hint of mockery in her tone. "And your invitation was just too intriguing to resist."

"I'm grateful," Ward said, enjoying the light-hearted banter. "But if word gets around you were out riding with me it won't do much for your reputation."

"Nor will it for yours," Priscilla said through a quick laugh, "especially if your employer hears about it." He gave her a questioning look. "I mean the female one," she added.

Ward felt suddenly awkward and wondered if he was

blushing. "Yeah, well . . . ah, that's . . . that's kind of what I wanted to talk to you about."

"How disappointing," Priscilla said, with an exaggerated pout. "I was hoping that perhaps you had something more . . . well, something more personal on your mind."

Ward was no longer sure she was joking. "Please," he said, "don't make this any harder than it is. But you're a woman . . ."

"How nice of you to notice," Priscilla shot back, her tone suddenly testy.

"You know what I mean," Ward replied, feeling the tension rise between them. This was not the way he had expected the conversation to go. "It's just that sometimes it takes a woman to understand another woman, and I just thought maybe you could . . ."

"What's to understand?" She gazed at him frankly, her green eyes glistening. "You're a man . . . a very attractive man. Either a woman has feelings for you, or she doesn't." Then after a short pause she said softly, "Is she in love with you?" There was an almost plaintive quality in her voice.

"You get right to the point, don't you?"

Pricilla reined up and Ward followed suit. "Well," she said, her voice turning cooler, more harsh, "is she in love with you?"

"She thinks she is."

"Are you in love with her?"

"I don't want her to get hurt."

"You didn't answer my question," she said icily.

Ward was surprised by the sudden change in Priscilla's mood. "If you loved a man," he said quickly, "wouldn't you want him to do what he had to do? Would you want him to change, to be less than a man?"

"Is that what you think makes you a man? Risking your life with a gun in your hand?" Pricilla paused, her eyes snapping. "Your Miss Wells certainly wouldn't think so." She took a deep breath and let it out slowly. "Neither would I, for that matter."

The anger in her eyes gave way to longing as she held his gaze with her own. "But if you want to know what I would do . . . if I loved a man . . . you're going about it the wrong way." The anger returned to her flashing eyes. She wheeled her horse violently, and with a quick stroke of her crop across his rump bolted off at a full gallop.

"Wait!" Ward called after her, momentarily shocked. Then he spurred the roan into action. It took him several hundred yards to overtake Pricilla, and as he pulled alongside her thundering mount he silently acknowledged her excellent horsemanship. He grasped the Tennessee Walker's bridle and wrestled him to a reluctant stop.

Pricilla's green eyes glared defiantly, and she threatened to strike Ward with her riding crop.

"Whoa," he said, raising an arm in defense, "hold on there. There's no need for that." Pricilla lowered the crop but continued to glare. "It's a good thing you're not carrying a six-shooter," Ward said, smiling at the idea of it. "I'd be in real trouble."

Pricilla failed to see the humor in his remark. "You may think that's funny," she said, her tone frigid, "but it so happens that I'm an excellent shot."

"If you can shoot like you ride, I believe it." Ward stroked her horse's neck and soothed him with a few quiet words. Then he turned again to Pricilla. "What did I say back there? I just wanted to know . . ."

Pricilla was calmer now, but her words still had a brittle edge. "You just don't get it, do you?"

"I guess not."

"Women in love are delicate creatures, Mr. Livery. They don't like sharing." Then with swipe of her crop she put her mount into a gallop once more and raced away.

Ward didn't follow her this time. He sat for a few minutes trying to make sense out of the last few minutes. Then, with a shake of his head, he spurred the roan into an easy lope back toward town. A deep melancholy settled over him as he rode. He had hoped that talking to Priscilla would help him better understand Mary, as well as help him understand his own feelings. There was no denying that he felt an attraction for her, an attraction that at times was strong. But was that love? Now, after Priscilla's outburst, he was more confused than ever.

Just forget it, Ward, he told himself. *Your gun hand's almost better. Another week or so and you can leave town and get to doing what you have to do.* But with that thought came a tiny nagging doubt from somewhere deep in his gut that he couldn't ignore. Was his gun hand really that much better? He wasn't so sure.

By the time he got back to town it was late afternoon. He put the roan up in the livery stable and started across the street to his room at the general store. He took off his gun belt and slung it over his shoulder. *Guess there's no need to keep it wrapped up in a cloth anymore,* he reminded himself. *It's not like it's a secret.*

As he crossed the street he glanced toward the saloon, wondering if Priscilla was in her office or at the bar and if she would still be so upset. A man was standing just inside the entrance, most of his face hidden behind the swinging doors. Only his eyes were visible above the slats, and his gaze followed Ward as he moved along the street. There was something familiar about the man's eyes; their look haunted Ward, and he probed deeply into his memory trying to recall where he had seen them before.

A harsh voice broke his concentration. "You're still here?"

Ward stopped and looked up as Travis Dutton came out of the general store, walked down the steps, and leaned against the hitch rail. "I thought I told you I wanted you out . . ." He paused, and his eyes bulged at the sight of the holstered revolver slung over Ward's shoulder. "That thing could get you into a lot of trouble."

Ward hung his rig over the hitch rail. "Trouble seems to have a way of finding me," he said, turning toward the sheriff, "with or without a gun."

"This is the last time I'm goin' to tell you, Ward . . ." Dutton's warning was interrupted by the clatter of the saloon doors bursting open. Ward turned at the sound and was just in time to see a man break across the wooden sidewalk and dive for a horse tied at the rail in front of the saloon. His rush scared the animal, and as he tried to swing up into the saddle the horse shied and backed away.

Ward wasn't sure he could believe his eyes. "Archer!" he shouted, and lunged for his six-shooter hanging on the rail. As he turned with the gun in his hand, Archer got his mount under control, swung into the saddle, and spurred the horse into a frantic gallop away from the saloon. "Hold it, Archer!" Ward yelled again and fired off two hasty shots, both of which missed their mark.

"Drop it, Ward!" Dutton barked over the receding clatter of the horse's hooves. Ward turned to see the sheriff's

gun pointed at his chest. "I said drop it. Hands in the air."
Ward let his weapon fall to the street and slowly raised his
hands. "Now," Dutton wanted to know, "what was that all
about?"

"Let me put my hands down and I'll tell you."

The sheriff nodded his cautious assent; then he motioned Ward back a few steps and picked up his six-
shooter, replaced it in its holster, and slung it over his
shoulder. He started toward the jail. "Tell me tomorrow
when you pick up your gun . . . on your way out of town."

Ward paid little attention to the sheriff's words. His
mind was on a question that was causing lengthening
fingers of doubt to send shivers along his spine. *How
could I have missed Archer with both shots?* he asked
himself—and for some reason he thought about Milt
Wells.

"Where's he stayin' in Purgatory?" Royce asked after
Clay Archer told him about his chance encounter with
Ward. They were sitting astride their horses in the long
shadows of late afternoon that were creeping across the
rolling hills on the outskirts of town.

"How do I know?" Archer replied. "All I know is he's
there. I just seen him not more than two hours ago. Ask
around. You want me to do all your work?"

"Don't get too cocky," Royce said, with an edge of
annoyance in his voice. He didn't like Archer's tone.

"No one asked you to do any work." Then, satisfied with the glint of fear that appeared in Archer's eyes, he added, "But it'll take me a few days."

"How come so long?" Archer whined. "I don't want him nosin' around the cattle again."

"The cattle's your problem. I've got to be careful not to scare him off. Now that we found him I don't want him leaving town."

"He ain't the scarin' kind," Archer replied.

Royce gave a short laugh. "We'll see about that." He wheeled his horse and paused to stare at Archer. "You take care of your cows. I'll take care of Mr. Ward." Then he touched spurs to his horse's flanks and loped off in the direction of Purgatory.

The next morning Ward was standing in the sheriff's office nursing a tin mug of bitter coffee. Dutton was seated with his feet propped up on his desk. He had a somber look on his face. "I just don't believe it, Ward. Archer's been foreman at the Kelso spread for years."

"Would you believe he's got two hundred head stashed up in Dry Canyon—waiting to be run down to Mexico?"

The sheriff's eyebrows formed twin arches over his bulging eyes. "You say he's got two hundred head? You're talkin' through your hat."

"Maybe there's more. He's got them spread all over."

Dutton's eyes narrowed. "How do you know so much about this?" he said suspiciously.

"My brother told me. Old Man Kelso hired him to find out who was rustling his beef. That's why he was in Mexico. And that's why I came back here after I found out he'd been killed. It turned into kind of a family thing. I'd been doggin' Archer for nearly a month before his men gunned me down in that dry wash."

Dutton scowled and gave Ward a skeptical look. "You expect me to take the word of a convicted murderer?"

"You don't have to take anyone's word for it. Take a ride with me, and I'll show you all the proof you need."

"What kind of proof are we talkin' about here?"

"It's the four-legged kind," Ward replied. He thought he saw a hint of worry replace the skepticism in Dutton's look, but it was gone before he could be sure.

"Okay," Dutton said, after a pause, "but this better be good." He got up from behind the desk and led the way toward the door.

"You know, there's one other thing, Sheriff."

Dutton stopped with his hand on the door latch.

"I want my gun back," Ward said, motioning to his rig hanging from a peg in the wall.

"I'm not sure I like the idea of you wearin' that thing," Dutton told him, "even though you ain't goin' to be here that long."

"I'm not sure I like the idea of being without it," Ward argued, "no matter how long I'm here."

Dutton rubbed his chin thoughtfully for a few seconds, then nodded. "I guess it can't hurt . . . long as it's no more'n a day or two." He watched through squinty eyes as Ward strapped on the gun belt. "That's a pretty fancy rig," he said.

"It was a present from my father. He gave one to me and one to my brother when we turned sixteen. We used to think they brought us luck," Ward said, feeling a sudden melancholy as he fingered the silver conch on the holster.

"Just see it don't get you killed too," Dutton said and opened the door and led them out to the street where their horses were tied up at the hitch rail.

The two men mounted up and rode out of town at a steady lope for a half hour until they came to a tree-lined hill overlooking a shallow valley. Ward signaled for them to stop and pointed to the valley floor to where a small, crude corral, partly hidden by trees, held a half dozen steers. The familiar scene brought back a rush of memories of gunplay and a frantic chase through the pines.

"I thought you said a couple hundred," Dutton scoffed, interrupting Ward's painful reverie. "There ain't more'n six or eight cows down there."

"I told you Archer has them spread all over," Ward replied and led the way down the hillside.

When they reached the corral Dutton dismounted and climbed through the rails. "I knew you were barkin' up the wrong tree," he said after he had examined part of the small herd. "These cows ain't wearin' the Kelso brand."

"Of course not," Ward told him, as the sheriff climbed out of the corral and back up onto his horse. "Archer re-brands them before he runs them down to Mexico."

"Well, well, you're some smart fellow, Ward." It was a voice from somewhere in the nearby trees.

Ward and Dutton whirled in their saddles to see Clay Archer, six-shooter in hand, riding slowly out of the pines in their direction.

"Archer!" Dutton barked. "What in blazes are you doing . . . ?"

"Hello, Travis," Archer said, leering, while he kept his gun leveled at Ward's chest. He reined up a few feet from the other two men. "Okay, you're right about the cows, Ward . . ."

"Heard enough, Sheriff?" Ward broke in. "Are you satisfied now? What more proof do you want?"

Archer's laugh was more of a cackle. "It looks like he figured out our little scheme, Travis," he said, before Dutton could answer.

"Shut your mouth, Archer!"

"Don't worry, Sheriff," Archer said through another nervous giggle. "He ain't goin' to live long enough to tell nobody."

"Now, hold on just a minute!" Dutton's voice was suddenly tinged with fear. "Lookin' the other way while you steal a few cows is one thing, but you're talkin' about murder. I don't want any part of it."

"No, no, you got it all wrong," Archer said, giggling again. "Me and you found Ward here rustlin' old man Kelso's beef. We tried to stop him, but he put up a fight and got killed."

"Are you crazy?" Dutton shot back.

"Naw, I'm just lucky is more like it. This way I get rid of Ward and get to save a bundle of money in the bargain."

"What're you talkin' about?"

Archer grinned. "Oh, it's just a little arrangement I had."

"No matter, it's still murder," the sheriff insisted.

"Well, if that's how you feel," Archer said, turning his gun on Dutton, "then I guess I can't leave no witnesses."

"You filthy double crosser!" The sheriff clutched at his six-shooter, but he was too late. Archer's Colt cracked in the stillness, and Dutton twisted out of his saddle and slammed to the ground.

Ward drew his own gun with all the quickness that he had and got off a rapid shot that missed. His second shot found its mark, and Archer slumped in his saddle but managed to hang on. As Ward was about to fire again, his horse reared, an action that probably saved his life as another shot from Archer tore into a corral post just inches from his head and sent splinters flying.

Then Archer spurred his horse, wheeled into a lurching gallop, and bolted back into the nearby trees.

Ward was about to give chase, but a groan from Dutton caused him to change his mind. He dismounted and went to the wounded sheriff. Blood soaked his shirtfront, but as Ward bent over him he could see that Dutton was not as seriously hurt as he first appeared. He helped him sit up and used Dutton's own neckerchief to help stanch the already slowing flow of blood.

"It seems as though you might have some explaining to do, Sheriff."

Some color began to return to Dutton's pallid face. "It's . . . it's not what you think, Ward," he responded weakly.

"Good," Ward said and helped him to his feet. "You can tell me all about it on the way back to town."

Chapter Eleven

Matt Hennessey sat with Livery at a corner table in the Irishman's restaurant, their hands wrapped around mugs of coffee and their heads close together so as to keep their voices from reaching the pair of lone diners across the room.

"How's the sheriff doin'?" Hennessey asked.

"He's coming along," Livery told him. "Milt Wells says he should be all right in a couple more weeks."

"So, what's his alibi?"

"He claims he's been working on the sly to get evidence against Archer."

"Fiddlesticks!" Hennessey exclaimed and drew a quick look from the diners. "You don't believe him, now do you?" he added softly.

"No. He's got all the evidence he needs—especially after what Archer said that day at the corral. But Dutton still hasn't called in the U.S. marshal."

"Ain't he takin' quite a chance? You could squeal on him anytime. So could Archer, for that matter."

"My guess is that the sheriff will try to kill Archer as soon as he gets the chance." Livery paused, grew thoughtful. "And he knows I'm not likely to run to the law real soon."

Hennessey shot him a quick look. "You mean you're not goin' to do anything about this?" He studied Livery's face for a moment. "It looks like we might be needin' a new sheriff before long, and I was just thinkin' maybe you might . . ."

"That's the town's problem," Livery interrupted, "not mine. Let me put it this way: I'm in a position now where I don't want to bother the sheriff and he doesn't want to bother me. Besides, I've got other business to take care of."

Hennessey was about to ask Livery to explain his curious comment about not wanting to bother the sheriff when one of the diners yelled for more coffee, and while the Irishman took care of his customer, Livery left the restaurant without saying good-bye. Matt went to the doorway and watched him cross over to the general store and disappear down the alley toward his room, and he wondered what the standoff between Livery and the sheriff was all about. *And,* he asked himself, *what was this other business he had to take care of?*

Hennessey casually eyed the few pedestrians moving along the main street between the riders and an occasional buggy. One of the horsemen caught his attention. He was tall and thin, and dressed all in black from his flat-crowned Stetson down to the boots that were adorned with silver spurs, their big Mexican rowels glinting in the sun. He sported an ivory-handled Colt in a holster slung low on his hip and tied down with a leather thong. Hennessey watched as the man stopped at the Red Dog Saloon, went quickly inside, then in minutes reappeared and mounted up again. Matt found it odd when the man repeated the action with stops at the livery stable, the stage depot, and the telegraph office, all in quick succession. It was only at the sheriff's office that his pattern differed. He dismounted and headed for the door, but obviously thought better of it and returned to his horse without going inside.

Then he headed for the general store.

Ward let himself into his room and crossed quietly to the door that led to the main part of the general store. He opened it a few inches and saw Mary, alone and arranging canned goods on one of the shelves. Since he was not in the mood for any lectures about guns and violence he thought it would save a lot of strife just to put his sidearm away. He unbuckled his gun belt, and as he was putting it in a bureau drawer he heard the thud of boots and the ching of spurs coming from the store. He went softly to the door again and peered through the narrow opening.

A tall, thin man dressed in black strode to the middle of the room. Mary looked as though she were carved in marble as the man studied her with a squinty gaze.

"Afternoon, Miss." The man's voice was soft but filled with menace.

"Can I help you?" Mary said in little more than a whisper. She put a hand to her cheek and shuddered.

"My name's Royce. I'm looking for a man named Ward. And since I'm sure everybody comes into your store sooner or later I thought . . ."

"Sorry," Mary replied, her voice stronger now, "I don't know anybody by that name." She moved so the counter was between her and Royce.

"He's about my age," Royce persisted, "and he wears a gun and fancy holster with a silver concho."

"I told you," Mary said, her voice suddenly strident, "I don't know any . . . !"

"There's no need to raise your voice, Miss. There's nothing wrong with my hearing."

"And there's nothing wrong with my eyesight. I've never seen any . . . any Ward . . . or whatever his name is."

From his position in the storeroom, Ward was mesmerized by the image of the tall stranger. He couldn't recall ever seeing such a picture of evil, even in the faces of the countless men he had gone up against in his past. Yet there was something vaguely familiar about the dark eyes and the thin, cruel-looking mouth. It was on the wanted poster—the one he had seen in Travis Dutton's office of a man wanted in Mexico for murder! Ward ran his hand along the hip where his gun should have been and thought about going to the bureau drawer. But he was frozen, transfixed.

"If he happens to come in," Royce said to Mary, "tell him I'd like to talk to him. I've got a room over at the saloon." Then he touched the brim of his hat and turned and swaggered slowly toward the front door.

"Mister, wait!" Mary took a few cautious steps from behind the counter then hesitated.

Royce stopped and turned, his hand resting on the butt of his Colt.

"This man," Mary asked, her voice cracking, "this Ward . . . is he . . . a friend of yours?"

"Let's just say we . . . let's say we know some of the same people."

Mary stood motionless, biting her lower lip, as she watched Royce go out the door to be lost in the sparse crowd moving along the street. Ward could see the worry lines in her face as he left the storeroom and started toward her. The door clicked shut behind him. Mary looked up at the sound, and there was a glint of fear in her eyes. Her gaze held his while an uneasy tension built between them. Then, in a hushed voice, she said, "It's him, isn't it? He's the one you're after."

Ward shrugged. "I don't know. It could be. I've never seen the man I'm looking for. All I know is that whoever it was killed my brother." He went to Mary and held her gently by the shoulders while her eyes searched his face.

"Who is Ward?" she whispered as a tear spilled down her cheek. "It's you, isn't it?" she went on when he didn't answer. "You're Ward."

"So now you know. What difference does it make?"

"What difference does it make?" she said, her voice rising as she stepped back from his touch. "The most evil-looking person I've ever seen in my life comes in here asking for a man named Ward . . . who turns out to be you . . . and you want to know what difference it makes?"

The front door opened and Milt Wells strode in, a smile on his face. He eyed the two people standing stiffly in the middle of the room and his smile turned to a frown. "Is anything wrong?"

"You should have seen him," Mary said her eyes snapping. "He looked positively . . . satanic!"

"Who are we talking about?"

"Your daughter's imagining things," Ward said. "There's just a man who wants to see me—a man I need to talk to."

"You wouldn't!" Mary said as her eyes widened and she put a hand to her mouth.

Milt frowned at her then turned to Ward. "What's this all about?"

"He could be the man who killed my brother."

"Walk softly, John," Milt said, suddenly concerned. "Are you sure this is the right thing to do?"

"I can't back away from it now."

"John," Milt persisted, "forget the past. You've made the beginnings of a new life here."

"Look, you've all got to accept the fact that I may be something . . . someone . . . you wouldn't like very much." He paused as a fleeting image of his brother appeared in his mind then disappeared. "No matter how much I may wish things had been different."

"You can be whatever you want to be," Mary said, a hint of irritation creeping into her voice.

"You make it sound so easy."

"I never said it was easy. But it's your choice. Just leave the past alone . . . whatever it was."

Ward sighed and studied his hands. "Sometimes things get started that can't be stopped."

"You don't want to stop, do you?" Mary sounded angry.

"I'm not sure it's up to me anymore," he said quietly. "That's why I've got to see this man." He felt suddenly weary, and the small, tormenting doubt began to nag at him again from somewhere deep inside. *What if he is the man I'm looking for?* he thought. *What if it comes to a showdown? Am I fast enough . . . ?* He didn't want to finish the thought, so without looking at Mary or her father, he started for the front door.

"Where are you going?" Mary said, but Ward didn't answer. "Dad" she went on, her voice pleading now, "Can't you do something?"

"John, don't be rash." Milt intercepted him at the door and put a gentle hand on his arm. "Let's talk this over."

"I've said all I have to say," Ward replied and removed himself from Milt's grasp. He went out the door, onto the board sidewalk, and quickly crossed the street to the saloon. It was empty except for a couple of old men at one of the tables and a faded beauty leaning against the bar talking to a bartender who was wiping imaginary spots off a glass. When he saw Ward he left the painted woman as though glad to get away from her.

"Yes sir, what can I get you?"

"You can help me find Royce."

The barman's brow wrinkled. "What did you say?"

"A man named Royce— he's staying here. What room is he in?"

"Oh, yes sir, I know who you want." The man pointed. "He's up the stairs, all the way to the back."

Feeling a mixture of excitement and apprehension, Ward quickly mounted the steps to the second floor and moved warily down a hallway lighted only by the feeble glow of a single lantern. He walked softly, but still he was conscious of the thud of his boots on the bare flooring. He stopped at the last door and listened. Then he knocked.

"Yeah?"

Ward wasn't sure he recognized the muffled voice as that of the man he had seen in the general store. "Royce?" he said.

"Who is it?"

Now he was sure. "It's the man you're looking for," he answered. There was silence for a moment, then the squeak of bedsprings and the thump of approaching footsteps and the soft jangle of spurs. The door opened slowly. Royce stood with one hand on the knob and the other holding his Colt pointed at Ward's chest. His lips moved in what might have passed for a smile except for the obvious cruelty in the rest of his face. He squinted into the weak light of the hallway trying to penetrate the shadows that fell across Ward's head and shoulders. Royce's eyes swept over Ward's hips, and when he saw he wasn't wearing a holster he let his gun hand fall limp at his side.

"Well, well," Royce said through a mirthless chuckle, "I never expected you to make my job so easy. I'm in your debt. Come in so I can get a good look . . ."

Ward stepped into the light of the room.

Royce recoiled as though stuck by a blow. "It's you! But you're . . . you're dead!"

Ward stared into Royce's face and bulging eyes. "What are you talking about?"

"I swear I killed . . ." he started, momentarily shaken. Then, quickly recovering his poise, he said, "Never mind. I . . . I thought you were someone else."

"Yeah," Ward said, suddenly angry, "I'm sure you thought I was someone else—like my brother. So you are the one." He ran his hand along his hip. "I've been looking for you for a long time."

"That makes us even," Royce snarled and raised his .45 again.

Ward held both hands away from his body and motioned toward Royce's gun. "You don't need that—not this time . . . unless you're the kind who'd shoot an unarmed man."

"I'd gladly kill you right now," Royce said, lowering his gun, "but I want you to worry for a while, to sweat a little."

Ward took a step back into the hallway. "I'll be coming for you, Royce."

The weak light from the lantern reflected yellow pinpoints of evil in Royce's eyes, and his strange giggle sent a chill down Ward's spine. "I can't wait," he hissed. "It'll be the first time I ever got paid twice for killing the same man."

Ward turned and retreated down the dim hallway with Royce's eerie laughter ringing in his ears. He left the saloon and crossed to the alley next to the general store and let himself into his room through the side door. With a vague doubt stirring again somewhere deep in his mind, he took his gun and holster out of the bureau and strapped it on. Then, with a vision of Royce's leering face whirling in his imagination, he crouched and drew with all the speed at his command. A derisive cackle echoed in his ears. "You've got to be a lot faster than that, Ward," the grinning image said just before it dissolved.

Maybe he's right, Ward thought, and rubbed at his shoulder and the old wound. *Maybe he's right.*

Chapter Twelve

Royce crossed the board sidewalk in front of the saloon and went down the steps to where his horse was tied up at the hitch rail. As he swung into the saddle he looked up to see Priscilla Scanlon come through the swinging doors. She had a small thin cigar in her hand and she stopped at the top step and put it to her red lips.

Royce admired her openly and she returned his gaze with an indifferent stare through the wisp of smoke that drifted lazily around her face. "Shame on you," he said, smiling, "smoking in public. Aren't you worried about your reputation?"

"It's a little late," Priscilla replied coolly. "That was ruined a long time ago."

"I know what you mean. We have something in common."

"I doubt it," she said and threw her cigar into the street and started along the sidewalk.

Royce laughed and turned his horse away from the saloon and headed out of town. He had sent word to

Archer that he wanted to meet, and now that Royce felt sure that Ward was not going to run, it was time to demand his money so he could get this job over with. He was already getting bored with Purgatory and was looking forward to the excitement of a showdown with Ward, although it didn't promise to be much of a fight. Royce could have killed him when he'd come to his room not wearing a gun, but that wasn't his style. He had never met a man he couldn't outdraw. And Ward would be no exception.

When he reached a small line shack a few miles out of town on the edge of the Kelso ranch, Royce tied up his mount next to the horse that was already at the rail. Inside, he found Archer seated at a small table set with a bottle of whiskey and some glasses. A clean white bandage peeked out through his open shirt collar. He looked up when Royce came in and motioned him to a chair.

"Why didn't you tell me it was Ward's twin brother I killed in Mexico?" Royce said as he sat down and poured himself a drink.

"I didn't know."

"They're the spitting image of each other."

"That ought to make it easier then," Archer said, smiling weakly, "seein' how's you've had the practice."

Royce didn't find the remark funny. "I need to get paid."

"We been through this before. I ain't too crazy about payin' for a job till it's finished."

Royce was surprised at Archer's bold tone, and concluded that it was probably the whiskey talking. "Look, Archer," he said, "as soon as I take care of Ward, I'm leaving town. And I don't want to have to come looking for you to get my money."

Archer poured himself another drink and his hand trembled slightly when he raised the glass to his lips.

"Of course, if *you* want to go up against him again," Royce added, and pointed at the other man's bandages, "you might have better luck next time."

Archer's tentative smile turned to a frown and he gulped at his drink. Then he reached into a shirt pocket, pulled out a handful of crumpled bills, and began to smooth them out on the table. "When're you goin' to do it?" he said, sounding suddenly impatient.

"Soon."

"It can't be soon enough for me," Archer said, and pushed the small pile of money in Royce's direction.

Ward was in a foul mood, and an early breakfast had done nothing to change it. He finished the last of his nearly cold coffee, pushed the cup away, and grumbled something to Matt Hennessey about not liking grounds in his teeth.

"I'm sorry about that, lad. Come lunchtime I'll give

you a free plate of stew to make up for it. How's that?"

Ward put some money on the counter and, without answering, left the restaurant and headed for the general store. Inside, Mary was folding blankets and arranging them on a shelf. She looked up and smiled, but he ignored her and headed directly for his room.

"You sleep all right last night?" she said just as he got to the storeroom door.

He paused with his hand on the latch. "I'm fine."

"Is something bothering you?"

"I just got things on my mind," he replied without turning to look at her.

Mary crossed to where he was standing and touched his arm lightly. "Sometimes it helps to talk."

"There's nothing to talk about," he said and gently removed her hand.

"It's that man, isn't it?" Mary said, peering intently into his face. "You went to see him last night."

Ward read the worry in her eyes, and stared back at her for what seemed like a long time. "He came to kill me," he said finally, his voice a husky whisper.

Mary sucked in a deep breath and her eyes grew wide. She shuddered and hugged herself as though suddenly chilled. "Can't . . . can't the sheriff do something?"

"It's none of his business," Ward snapped, his tone gruff. "I'll handle it."

"How will you handle it—by getting killed?" She touched his arm again.

"Mary, I know how you feel," he said, his voice growing more gentle, and he covered her hand with his. "But there's something else. This man killed my brother."

Mary's eyes widened again but her voice was firm when she said, "Is fighting going to bring him back? It only means more killing. Even if you win, you lose. Can't you see that?"

"You don't understand," Ward insisted. "This man's a professional killer. My brother wasn't a gunfighter. He never had a chance."

Mary scowled. "How do you know? You weren't there."

"I know because"—Ward hesitated—"I know because I'm . . . I know his kind. Believe me, I know."

"Even so, do you have to answer violence with violence? Is that what you want?"

"I want justice," he answered.

Mary's eyes snapped. "Is it really justice you want— or revenge?" Then her look turned to pleading and she took his hand in both of hers. "Oh, John, let it go— please. It takes two people to make a fight. He's powerless if you just ignore him." She squeezed his hand as if to emphasize her words. "Promise me you'll . . . just promise that you'll at least think about it."

He wanted to answer her, but he couldn't. He suddenly found himself wondering if she was right, then put the thought out of his mind. He had to do this thing for his brother. An awkward silence grew between them; then he pulled his hand from Mary's grasp and pushed through the door to his room and slammed it behind him. He went to the bureau, took out his empty six-shooter and held it in his hand, just looking at it. *Maybe there is a better way,* he thought. *What if she's right?* Then he strapped on his gun belt and slipped the Colt into the holster. He drew swiftly, as though facing a mortal enemy, and squeezed the trigger. The click of the hammer falling on an empty chamber was loud in the small room. Ward took satisfaction from the fact that most of the pain was gone from his shoulder. Only one question still nagged at him: was he fast enough yet? But after talking to Mary he couldn't help but wonder if he was really doing this thing for his brother or— or because of some deeply selfish reason, because of his need to prove to himself that he was good enough to beat Royce at his own game. Besides, after some thought, he had a pretty good idea why Royce had killed his brother and now wanted to kill him. It all had to do with Archer. Mary's words crept back into his mind. *Is fighting going to bring him back? It only means more killing. Even if you win, you lose. Can't you see that?*

He took off the gun belt and returned it to the drawer. Moving quietly, he crossed to the door that opened onto the alley and let himself out. With a few swift paces he covered the ground to the saloon and pushed through the swinging doors. The place was empty except for a couple of early morning drunks. He motioned to the sleepy bartender.

"Is Royce in his room?"

"No, sir, he ain't. I think he said he was goin' for breakfast over to the Irishman's restaurant."

Ward retraced his steps and crossed the street to Hennessey's. Matt was behind the counter, smiling as he surveyed the crowded tables. His smile widened when he saw Ward. "John, me boy," he bellowed. "Good to see you again. But you're a little early. The stew ain't ready yet. How 'bout a cup of coffee? There'll be no grounds this time, I promise."

"None for me right now." Ward scanned the crowd until he spotted Royce, sitting alone finishing his breakfast. He crossed to the table, pulled out a chair, and sat down.

Royce looked up, mildly surprised, but continued to eat. "Have a seat," he said through a mouthful of food.

"I know who sent you, Royce."

Royce shrugged and washed down his food with coffee. The eyes under the brim of his black Stetson narrowed to wary slits.

"It didn't take much to figure it was Archer," Ward added.

"Aren't you a smart man?"

"I'm smart enough to know there's got to be a better way to handle this than spilling blood."

Royce sneered. "I like it the way it is."

"There's been enough killing. More won't change the past. I don't want to fight you."

"It won't be much of a fight," Royce answered slowly, then slurped at the dregs of his coffee.

"My quarrel's with Archer," Ward persisted.

Royce pushed his plate away. "Don't think you can talk your way out of it, Ward," he snarled, his voice suddenly cold, taunting. "I've already been paid to kill you. And I always earn my pay."

"This isn't your business anymore."

"You spineless pup!" Royce thrust himself back from the table and his chair clattered to the floor. "At least your brother died like a man. But you . . . you come around here whining and sniveling, trying to save your worthless life!" He reached across the table, grabbed Ward by the shirt, and pulled him to his feet and off balance. "If you were wearing a gun," he hissed, "I'd . . ."

"Don't let that stop you," Ward growled, regaining his footing. Royce gave him a backhanded slap across the mouth and he tasted blood.

Some of the women customers screamed and, along with several men, scrambled for the door while others pressed against the walls of the restaurant.

Royce drew back his hand again, but before he could strike, Ward threw a short, quick punch to his chin and Royce tumbled backward onto his overturned chair. He bounced to his feet with the nimbleness of a cat and in the same motion drew his gun.

More screams and yells from the retreating customers brought Hennessey from the kitchen on the run. "Hey! We'll have none of that!" he bellowed from behind the counter, as he reached down and came up with a double-barreled shotgun. He pointed it at Royce and cocked both hammers. "Lest you want a little buck-shot for dessert, bucko, I'd suggest you put that thing away and just move along quietly." He motioned toward the door. "Breakfast is on me."

The commotion of seconds before was replaced by a tense silence. Royce glared at the Irishman, then turned his gaze on Ward. Slowly and deliberately, he eased his gun back into its holster. "Nothing will save you, Ward," he said, his tone flat and void of emotion. He strolled casually to the front door, stopped, and turned. With a mocking grin on his face he pointed at Ward, his fore-finger and raised thumb forming a pretend weapon. "Next time, gun or no gun, nothing will save you." The hammer on the make-believe gun fell silently, its evil intent clear, and Royce turned and swaggered out of the restaurant.

The room seemed to let out its breath and the few remaining customers began to whisper among themselves and steal glances in Ward's direction. Hennessey righted the overturned chairs and sat down, the shotgun across his lap. He gave Ward a quizzical look and motioned him to a seat. "What was that all about, if you don't mind me askin'?"

Ward sighed, then slumped into a chair. "It's a long story."

"We Irish are a patient lot." Matt eased the hammers down on the shotgun, laid it on the table, and leaned back in his chair.

Ward propped his elbows on the table. "My name's not Livery. It's Ward." Matt's forehead wrinkled but he didn't speak. "I'm wanted by the authorities," he went on. "I was convicted of murdering a man down in Mexico."

Hennessey's eyes narrowed. "I'd've never taken you for the murderin' kind."

Ward wasn't listening. "I was in a cantina down across the border," he said softly, "looking for my brother." He stared into his hands, hardly aware he was speaking. "A girl at the bar said she had seen a man who looked just like me. So I bought her a drink. But before I could get her to tell me anything, her boyfriend came in—a big guy, mean and looking for trouble. He started to push her around, and then he came after me, so . . ."

"You got in a fight," Hennessey volunteered.

Ward nodded. "I tried to explain, but he wouldn't listen. I told him I wasn't interested in the girl, but my Spanish isn't that good, and things . . . well, things got out of hand. He went for his gun."

"And he was second best," Hennessey said, and Ward nodded again. "Sounds to me like it was a fair fight."

"Except now the girl's screaming I killed her lover, and the next thing I know the *Federales* are there. They're in no mood to listen to an explanation, especially from a gringo—so I'm charged with murder." Ward paused, remembering. "The trial was short and sweet, Mexican-style. Next thing I know, I'm in a cell with a lone window looking out on a brand new scaffold they were building."

"At least you had a window," Hennessey said, grinning broadly. "Then what happened?"

"I managed to break out just before I was due to hang."

Hennessey leaned forward, elbows on his knees. "That explains you callin' yourself John Livery, but what about your brother?"

"He was an undercover lawman. We were twins. But we . . . we drifted apart years ago. I thought maybe if I could find him, we could . . . maybe we could patch things up, make up for lost time. But while I was in the

Mexican prison I heard he'd been killed. I've been trying to find the man who did it."

Hennessey's eyebrows arched. "And?" he asked.

"He found me."

"You mean the man who was just here?" Ward nodded. "So now what?" Hennessey wanted to know.

"He wants a showdown," Ward replied solemnly.

"You think you can take him?"

Ward pushed away from the table and stood up. "There's only one way to find out," he said and, ignoring the stares of the few remaining customers, headed for the door, leaving Hennessey alone with his shotgun.

Chapter Thirteen

Ward was still fuming over the memory of how Royce had slapped him in the face. Gun or no gun, it was the first time he had ever let anyone manhandle him and get away with it. He took his six-shooter and holster out of the bureau and, as he strapped it on, he vowed to himself it would never happen again. He grabbed his Stetson off the bedpost and was about to let himself out onto the street when a soft click of the door to the main store caused him to stop and turn.

Mary stood framed in the doorway. Her mouth was drawn into a tight line and her eyes roamed over the gun on his hip. "Why are you doing this?" she said quietly. It was more of a plea than a rebuke.

Ward was tempted to tell her what had happened at Hennessey's, to try to explain once again how he felt and that he was convinced now more than ever of what he had to do. Instead he just said, "I tried your way. It didn't work." Then he turned and left. Once out in the street he went to the front of the general store to where his horse was standing at the hitch rail.

As he was about to climb into the saddle a voice called out, "Ward!"

He turned to see Travis Dutton approaching. Dutton walked up and leaned an arm on Ward's saddle and peered at him through narrowed eyelids. "I expected you to be movin' on by now," he said.

"I've got unfinished business."

"Finish it someplace else," the sheriff growled. "We don't want your kind around here."

Ward brushed Dutton's arm out of the way and swung up onto his horse. "Don't push your luck, Sheriff. Given what I know about your dealings with Archer, you might want to stay on my good side."

"Don't threaten me, Ward. You got no proof I ever had anything to do with Archer."

"Maybe I do, and then again maybe I don't." Ward moved his horse away from the hitch rail. "But if I were you, I wouldn't want the U.S. marshal looking into it anytime soon, so you might want to cut me some slack."

Dutton scowled, and a hint of fear showed in his eyes.

"Think it over," Ward said and touched his spurs to his horse's flanks.

A few minutes later he reined up in front of the church,

dismounted, and went inside. The nave was empty and the thud of his boots and the jangle of spurs shattered the silence as he went directly to the small pulpit. He stood for a moment with his head bowed.

"I thought this wasn't for you."

Ward looked up to see Milt Wells crossing the nave from a side door. "It's not what you think."

Milt glanced at Ward's Stetson. He smiled and his kindly eyes twinkled. "We usually take off our hats in here."

"Your place. Your rules." He removed his hat and stood holding it in front of him with both hands.

"I was hoping you'd come back," Milt said. "I had a feeling you might find what you're looking for in here." He made a sweeping motion with his arm and gazed quickly around the small church. "I'm glad you gave it another chance."

"You might not be when I tell you why."

Milt's smile turned to a quizzical look.

"I need help," Ward said.

"That's why most people come here," Milt replied, and his smile returned.

Ward reached behind the pulpit and came up with Milt's gun belt. "Let's go outside," he said in answer to Milt's puzzled look. Milt followed him out the door and he led them to the partially wooded grassy area in back of the church, where he stopped and handed the preacher his six-shooter. "Put this on, will you?"

Milt let the gun belt hang limply by one hand. "Now wait, I told you . . ."

"You said people come here for help," Ward interrupted.

"What's that got to do with me strapping this thing on again?"

"You'll see." Ward picked up two rocks, each about half the size of a man's fist, and went to a fallen log twenty feet from where they were standing. He set the rocks on the log about a yard apart.

"What's this all about?" Milt wanted to know.

Ward took out his Colt and spun the cylinder. "That stranger in town, Royce—he came here to kill me."

Milt's face blanched. "Good grief! Have you told Travis?"

"He's got his own problems." Ward holstered his weapon. "What I need is to know if I'm fast enough to take him."

"And you want me to . . . ?" Milt couldn't finish his thought.

Ward finished it for him. "I want you to help me get ready."

"John, John, you know how I feel about this."

Ward held up a hand. "Let me put it this way. I'm going to have to fight him one way or another. If you're so against killing, help me save a life"—he paused and stared into Milt's lined face—"mine."

The creases deepened around Milt's eyes—eyes that were suddenly filled with pain. He shook his head slowly. "This is foolishness. It's out of the question."

"Just so you know, Royce killed my brother."

Milt's brow wrinkled, and he seemed deep in thought. "Was it a fair fight?"

"Who knows? My brother was fast, but he was no gunfighter."

Milt chewed on his bottom lip and shook his head as though answering some unasked question. "This is madness," he whispered.

"You know Mary loves me, Milt. You said so yourself. I never wanted it, but there it is. There's nothing I can do about it." Milt nodded and hung his head for a moment. "Maybe you'd be helping save her some grief," Ward added.

Milt glanced up quickly, his face dark. Then his look softened. He sighed and looked toward heaven, and without speaking began to strap on his gun belt. "Let's see how quick you are."

Ward smiled.

"Mind you," Milt added quickly as he tied his holster to his leg, "I make no promises."

Ward pointed to the rocks on the log. "I'll count to three. You take the one on the left."

Milt shrugged out of his frock coat and limbered up the fingers on his right hand. Then he settled into a slight crouch, glanced at Ward, and nodded.

Ward counted to three, a shot rang out, and the rock on the left shattered into a puff of dust. A fraction of a second later—but long enough for a man to die—another shot pulverized the rock on the right. The two men stood side by side for a second, huddled statues frozen in time, their guns smoking, the smell of gunpowder filling the clear air.

Then Milt straightened up and holstered his six-shooter. His look was somber. "When do you have to fight this man?"

Ward holstered his weapon. "That'll be his call, but I expect it to be soon—very soon."

Milt flexed his fingers and rubbed his hands together. "Then, God help me," he said, "let's get started. We've got some work to do."

Mary set the evening meal on the table for her and her father, and a gloomy stillness settled over the room. She moved some food around on her plate but had no real interest in eating.

"Want to talk about it?" Milt asked finally, breaking the silence.

"Oh, Dad," Mary said and threw her fork clattering into her plate, "why can't I make him see how stupid it

is to fight this man? Why can't I make him understand?"

Milt nodded but avoided Mary's look. He cleared his
throat a few times, then said, "You sure he's the only
one that needs to understand things?"

Mary glanced at him sharply. "What's that supposed
to mean?"

Milt cleared his throat again. "I just . . . I'm just suggesting maybe we ought to consider John's feelings. Have
you given any thought to what he may be going through?"

"Well . . . yes, of course I have. I know it must be . . .
well, difficult for him."

"He's about to put his life on the line—against a professional gunman, from what I hear."

"That's my point exactly," Mary shot back.

"Look at it this way," Milt persisted. "You're asking
a proud man to run from a fight."

"How can you say that?" Mary said, her voice rising.
"You know how I feel about fighting and killing—about
violence. I'm not asking him to run, as you put it, just
to stay out of it."

"Isn't that the same thing in this case?" Milt answered softly.

The room settled into an uncomfortable silence once
more. Then, in a whisper, Mary said, "I'm so afraid, Dad.
I don't want him to get . . ." There was a catch in her
voice. "If only I could make him listen." Milt went to her

and pulled her gently to her feet and enfolded her in his arms. "I don't know what to do," Mary whispered. "I've been praying until my knees hurt."

"Then don't give up."

Mary looked up into her father's gentle face, surprised at his words.

"If that's how you feel, go to him. Lord knows I can't tell you what choice he should make, but if you care for him as much as I think you do, you'll find a way to get him to listen." Milt paused, and his slight smile looked sad. "And believe me, I'd like nothing better."

Mary wiped at a stray tear. "Do you mean what I think you mean?"

Milt nodded, and his smile grew wider.

"Now?" she said. "Go to him now?"

"Why not?"

Mary couldn't contain a small laugh. She hugged her father, then spun away from his embrace. "Then help me clear the table!"

"But you didn't touch your food," Milt protested.

"Who cares about eating?" Mary said with a laugh, and grabbed some dishes and started for the kitchen. She paused and looked back at her father. "And, Dad . . . thanks."

Priscilla Scanlon came out of the Red Dog Saloon into the early dark of evening and paused at the steps leading down from the wooden sidewalk. She took the shawl from around her shoulders and placed it over her head, then hurried across the deserted street and down the alley beside the general store. She stopped at John Livery's door and tapped lightly.

He answered her knock and the weak light from his room lit up the startled look on his face. "Well, this is a surprise. After our little . . . what should I call it? Let's just say that after our ride the other day, I never expected to . . . well, I'm a little surprised to see you, that's all. Would you like . . . ah," he stammered, "to, ah . . . come in?"

Priscilla spoke quickly. "No, I just wanted to apologize for . . . well, for the way I acted that day. You asked me for help, and I behaved like a fool."

Livery shrugged. "Ask a dumb question . . ."

"It wasn't a dumb question. Do you remember what you said?"

"I asked if you'd try to change a man if you loved him."

Priscilla moved closer and put a hand on his arm. "And the answer's simple: yes. I'd do whatever it took to keep him from getting killed." She moved her hand to his cheek. "And if you're wise, you'll do what she wants you to do. Forget this man, Royce."

"It's not that simple," he replied.

"Find a way—somehow." Priscilla slipped her hand

behind his head and drew his face to hers. She crushed her mouth to his and kissed him long and deeply. Then she stood back, her breathing quick and shallow now, and stared into his eyes. "And be grateful," she said breathlessly, "that you've got someone who loves you as much as she does. And just know that, yes, if I loved a man that much I would do anything to save him— even risk my own life." She kissed him again, fiercely and quickly, then whirled and started out of the alley. After a few steps she paused in the darkness, listening. There was a sound like sobbing. Then a form emerged from the shadows, hardly more than a blur, giving Pricilla a fright. Whoever it was ran quickly out of the alley and disappeared around the corner.

Priscilla shivered, then pulled the shawl tighter around her shoulders and scurried back toward the saloon.

Milt settled into the easy chair that dominated the living room and shook open the newspaper. Just as he started to read, he heard a door slam on the floor below, then footsteps pounding on the stairs. Mary swept into the room, her face drawn and her mouth set in a tight line. There were tears on her cheeks.

He lowered the paper. He noticed the desolate look on his daughter's face. "Mary, what is it?" he said, as she breezed past without even a glance in his direction and went to her room and slammed the door. He slapped the paper against the arm of the chair with a loud whack. "Damnation!" he growled to the empty room.

It was as close as he had come to swearing in years.

Chapter Fourteen

The small stand of cottonwoods echoed with the sound of gunfire and the smell of cordite hung heavy on the still air. Milt and Livery stood side by side and blazed away with their six-shooters at a profusion of cans and bottles lined up on a fallen log some twenty feet distant. As glass shattered and cans spun crazily into the air, there were no misses.

They paused to reload. "We'll soon be out of bottles, John," Milt said as they flushed the empty shells out of the cylinders and refilled them, "not to mention bullets."

"I thought maybe you might have started calling me Ward by now," Livery said, "since my real name's no secret anymore."

"Oh, I know. But I've kind of gotten used to John Livery. It's a good name . . . to go with a good man." Milt smiled warmly. "My daughter likes it too."

"It's your choice," Livery said with a shrug. "But you can't change what your are—no matter what name you put on it."

"We should talk about that sometime," Milt said patiently, and then they holstered their guns. Milt stooped to pick up a tin can at his feet. "Let's go one more time," he said, glancing at Livery. "Are you ready?"

He nodded and Milt threw the can high in the air. In a blur of motion, Livery had his gun in hand and, with a succession of shots so rapid that the noise was almost like one continuous sound, kept the can spinning high overhead until he was out of bullets.

Then, while he reloaded, Milt set two small rocks about a foot apart on the log. "All right, now it's final exam time," he said with a grim look on his face, as he walked back to where the other man waited.

Livery flexed his fingers and both men faced the log. "You're on the left," he said.

Milt nodded. "Let's go on three," he replied, and the men crouched, hands over their guns, as intent as if they were facing live opponents. Before the sound of the three-count died, a shot rang out and the rock on the right exploded into fragments and dust. Smoke curled from the muzzle of Livery's revolver. Milt's hand was on his gun but he had not yet cleared leather. Still in a crouch, he stared at Livery and shook his head slowly from side to side, then let his weapon slip back into its holster.

"I saw it," Milt said softly, "but I still don't believe it. You're the fastest thing I've ever come across."

Livery accepted the compliment with a shrug. "There's just one problem," he said. "Rocks and cans don't shoot back. It's different when you're facing a man. I think you know that." He reloaded his gun and started away slowly.

Milt watched him go, pondering the truth of his words. He decided to see if Livery was right. He crouched again, hand poised over his holster. "Draw, Ward!" he barked.

Livery spun and in a split-second blur his six-shooter was in his hand pointing at Milt's chest before the older man could get his gun out of its holster. They stood staring at each other—and though it had been a sham contest, the air was filled with tension. Milt felt a rivulet of sweat run down his ribs as he let out a deep breath and tried to relax.

"You're ready, John. God forgive me, but you're ready."

Milt stood at the entrance to his church smiling and greeting the Sunday worshippers as they filed out.

Matt Hennessey and Mary came out the door, and the Irishman paused to shake the preacher's hand. "That was another good sermon, Milt."

"I'm not sure everyone in the family agrees with you." Milt glanced to where Mary stood waiting, looking disinterested and with her face drawn into a frown. "Was the preaching that bad, Mary?"

"I'm sorry," she said, trying to force a smile that

didn't make it. "It's just . . . I guess I'm just in a bad mood."

"It wouldn't have anything to do with John not being here, now would it?"

Mary's look grew more stern. "What *he* does is his own business. It has nothing to do with me."

"Well," Milt said, "when you get back to the store, tell him I said he could still use some help." Mary gave him a quizzical look. "He'll know what I mean," Milt added.

"He may not be at the store," Mary said as she started down the steps. She stopped and looked back. "Last time I saw him he was getting ready to pack his things." Then, with Hennessey trailing behind, she continued down the steps and headed toward town. Milt felt troubled. He watched his daughter and Matt until they were out of sight, then started back into the empty church.

"Milt!"

He turned to see Livery approaching on horseback from out of a nearby stand of trees at the side of the church.

The Red Dog Saloon was nearly empty, except for the two scruffy cowboys at one end of the bar talking to the bartender. Royce was at the other end of the bar. He sipped at the glass of whiskey in his hand, then refilled it from the bottle in front of him. The bartender ambled in his direction and began wiping up invisible spots with his bar towel.

"It's kind of quiet around town," he volunteered.

Royce gave him a cold look. The last thing he was interested in was useless conversation.

"There ain't much happenin' on a Sunday," the bartender persisted.

"I don't recall asking," Royce growled.

"Are you goin' to be around long?" the bartender said through a lopsided grin that revealed a missing front tooth.

Royce refilled his glass and sipped at it. Then he set it down carefully and gave the man a long, hard stare. "You running a saloon or a newspaper?"

"Hey, I'm just tryin' to be friendly."

"Don't try."

The bartender pouted and resumed wiping the unseen spots. Then he looked up and smiled. "What line of work are you in?"

Royce sighed, shook his head slowly, and chuckled. He had met his match. "I'm sort of a . . . hunter. Yeah, that's it, I'm a hunter." He drained his glass and slapped some coins on the bar.

"Y'ain't leavin', are you?" the bartender said hastily, with a woeful look on his face.

"I can't stand the excitement," Royce replied dryly.

The man brightened. "Wait till tomorrow. Things'll be boomin' again."

"You can count on it," Royce said and headed for the stairs that led up to his room.

From where she sat by the kerosene lantern trying to concentrate on her sewing, Mary glanced up as Milt sat back in his easy chair, lit his pipe, and opened his accounts ledger. Sunday evening was usually the time when he went over his records of the previous week's business. He glanced over at Mary and she smiled. She had gotten over her surly mood of earlier in the day, but she couldn't keep her mind on her sewing; her thoughts kept returning to John Livery—and how worried she was about him . . . and how she couldn't get used to thinking of him as someone named Ward.

She jabbed herself with the needle and the sudden pain shocked her back to the reality of the moment. "Oh, darn!" she cried and threw her sewing into the basket at her feet. She stood up and went to the window and sucked on her injured finger. She had an idea, but she wasn't sure she had the courage to carry it out. After a moment she heaved a deep sigh and turned to her father. "I'm going for a walk."

"That sounds like a good idea. For a minute there, I was afraid you were going to sew your fingers together."

Mary ignored his faint smile and the teasing glint in his eyes and took her cape from the coat rack by the stairs.

Outside, the dark street was deserted, and she pulled her cape close around her shoulders and walked quickly toward the Red Dog Saloon. Once inside, she looked neither right nor left but headed straight to the bar. Fighting back the impulse to turn and run from this place, she approached the bartender, who was talking to a dancehall girl.

When he saw Mary his eyes bulged and he turned away from the painted floozie. "Why, Miss Wells, this is the first time I ever seen you in here!"

Mary felt her cheeks burning. "I . . . is Miss Scanlon here tonight?"

"Priscilla?" The man pointed to a closed door just beyond the end of the bar. "Sure, she's in her office—right through that door."

"Would she . . . ? Do you think she'd mind if I . . . ?"

"Heck, no, not you, Miss Wells—just knock and go on in."

Trying to ignore the curious glances of the few scruffy patrons along the bar, Mary went to the office door and knocked softly.

"Come in," said a muffled voice from behind the door. "It's open."

Mary opened the door to a small neat office, and

found Priscilla seated at a rolltop desk that dominated the room. She looked up from the stack of papers in front of her and her eyebrows raised and she smiled pleasantly. "Why, Mary, come in." She motioned to a chair next to the desk. "Please sit down."

"No, thank you," Mary answered, trying to control the slight tremor in her voice, and closed the door from prying eyes. "I'll only be a minute."

"This is such a nice surprise," Priscilla said. "As many times as I've been in your place, I never expected you'd ever be in mine. Please do take a seat." She motioned to the chair again.

Mary ignored the gesture. "I never imagined I would come here, either, frankly. It's not . . ." She groped for the right words.

"It's not your kind of place?" Priscilla volunteered.

Mary sensed the warmth rising again in her cheeks and felt an urge to speak quickly. "Let me come right to the point."

Priscilla shrugged. "You've got the floor."

"I'm in love with John Livery," Mary blurted.

"How nice for you," Priscilla said without emotion, and with a sudden lack of warmth in her voice.

"I'm afraid he's going to . . . to fight a hired gunman, and I'm afraid he'll be killed."

"What does that have to do with me?" Priscilla said, her face a blank mask.

"I came here to ask you to stop him."

"How do you propose I do that?"

"I think he's . . . in love with you." Priscilla laughed, but Mary could detect no humor in her look. "I know you . . . I know you've been seeing him." Mary's heart beat rapidly and she squeezed her hands together to keep them from trembling.

"John Livery is a man," Priscilla said, her voice cool now. "He'll do what he chooses."

"But you can . . . You have ways to . . . to *persuade* him, to get him to change his mind." Mary felt like her cheeks were on fire. "Ways that I can't . . . I mean ways that I couldn't . . ."

Priscilla's eyes snapped and she sat straighter in her chair. "You mean I have ways that are all right for a saloon hussy, but too good for a *respectable* woman, is that the idea?"

Mary felt like she wanted to run. "No," she insisted, "that's not it at all. I only meant . . ."

Priscilla got to her feet. "I know exactly what you meant, Miss Wells." She went to the door and jerked it open. "What were you going to do, offer me money?"

Mary edged toward the open door. "No, of course not."

"That's the usual arrangement for what you're suggesting, isn't it?"

Mary was nearly blinded by embarrassment, at a loss

for words. Her heartbeat pounded in her ears. "Please, I . . . I didn't mean . . ."

Priscilla opened the door wider. "You're the one in love with him, Miss Wells. You *persuade* him, as you so nicely put it. You might find it . . . interesting."

The words struck Mary like a slap in the face. She stiffened, squared her shoulders, and stumbled toward the door. She paused for just a moment to peer into the other woman's face. Tears began to creep down Pricilla's cheeks and she bit at her lower lip to keep it from trembling.

"I'm sorry," Mary whispered. "I . . . I shouldn't have come." Then she swept past Priscilla and out of the saloon.

Royce turned up the kerosene lamp on the stand beside his bed and the flickering yellow light filled his small room. He sat on the bed and poured whiskey from a half-filled bottle into a glass and sipped at it. Then he took his six-shooter out of the holster hanging from the bedpost and, using a corner of the bed sheet, gently polished the gray-blue metal until it gleamed dully in the soft light. He ran his fingers over the steel, and its cold smoothness stirred him as much as if he were caressing the flesh of a woman. He pointed the weapon at some unseen target and his finger tightened around the trigger. He chuckled, almost giddy at the image that formed in his mind.

"Your time's up, Ward," he said softly, then returned the gun to its holster. Just as he started to unbutton his shirt, there was a soft tapping at the door. He quickly eased his gun out of the holster again and silently cocked the hammer.

"Yeah?"

"May I come in?" It was Priscilla.

He moved quietly to the door and eased it open. The weak light emphasized the coppery highlights in Pricilla's hair and reflected in her eyes. It was the first time Royce had paid attention to how pretty she was. He was suddenly charmed by her beauty. "Kind of late to be checking on your guests, isn't it?" he said as his gaze roamed over the curves of her body.

Priscilla eyed the gun in his hand and gave him a questioning look.

"One can never be too careful," Royce explained and slipped his gun into its holster. He motioned her into the room and stood admiring her in the soft light.

"Aren't you going to offer a lady a drink?"

"*Lady?*"

"You don't have to be nasty."

Royce poured whiskey in a glass and handed it to her. "You're a lady like I'm a gentleman."

Priscilla sipped at the whiskey. "Maybe you're right. We do have certain things in common."

Royce grabbed her roughly around the waist and pulled her close, causing her to spill her drink. She stiffened momentarily, then relaxed and fended him off with a hand against his chest. "Yeah," he said, a laugh rumbling deep in his throat, "our services are available to anyone. All it takes is money."

Priscilla twisted out of his grasp and added more whiskey to her glass. "There are things besides money."

"Name one," Royce said as she glided back to his side and ran a hand provocatively along his cheek.

"I might consider a trade," she purred, "a favor for a favor."

"What kind of favor?" Royce moved closer, his head almost touching hers, and he inhaled the faint aroma of rose water.

"I'm thinking something simple," she murmured. "Use your imagination."

She pushed him away gently, and Royce went to the bedside stand and poured more whiskey in his glass. He sipped at it slowly and eyed Pricilla over the rim of his glass.

She stared back coolly, then after a long pause said, "Well?"

"What do I have to do for this . . . this *trade*?"

"All you have to do," she said, taunting him with her eyes and a wry smile, "is to leave town. Get out of Purgatory."

"Yeah, yeah," he grunted, "in a day or two."

"No," she insisted, "it has to be tomorrow—first thing."

"I can't," Royce said and took a long drink of whiskey. "Maybe the day after."

Priscilla's smile faded and her look grew cold. She started for the door. She paused with her hand on the doorknob and turned toward Royce. "It's tomorrow morning or forget it."

Royce hesitated briefly, then downed the rest of his drink. "Okay, okay. Tomorrow morning it is, then." He started toward her.

"Wait," Priscilla said, stopping him with an upraised hand. "Just so we understand each other—you leave first thing tomorrow, agreed?"

Royce nodded eagerly.

Chapter Fifteen

Early Monday morning Milt made a last check of his ledger while Mary dusted the store's shelves in preparation for the week's business. He glanced up when the door to the storeroom opened and Livery came into the main store area. Milt was glad to see that he wasn't wearing his six-shooter. That would have only made Mary's mood worse, and she was already testy enough as it was.

"Good morning," Livery said. Milt nodded as Mary looked around, then quickly turned away without speaking. The atmosphere in the room was suddenly frigid. Livery examined his fingernails for a few moments then, looking awkward, said, "Just thought I'd see if there was anything you needed me to do—you know, before I leave. . . . There's not much time left and I'm all packed."

Mary turned again and gave him a long, cold stare. Milt bent lower over his ledger, determined not to do or say anything that would set his daughter off on another lecture about violence. Livery looked at him and shrugged, as if to say "What did I do?" When Milt didn't respond, Livery walked to where Mary had resumed her dusting.

"Okay, let's get this out in the open. You're sore because I didn't go to church with you yesterday, right?" His question was greeted with another icy stare. "Oh, I know. You heard I went riding with Priscilla Scanlon." Mary turned back to her dusting. "Well then, what is it?"

She wheeled around and threw the dust cloth down on the counter. "You really don't know, do you?"

"No! What's bothering you?"

"It just doesn't occur to you, does it, that I might be absolutely sick with fear—worried that you could be killed in the next day or two. How can you pretend that every thing is all right . . . ?"

The sound of the front door being flung open stopped her speech. All eyes turned as Royce walked into the store, a brazen smirk on his face. Mary's hand went to her mouth. "Oh, dear God!" she gasped.

Royce took a few swaggering steps, then stood with his hands on his hips, and his lips curled into a sneer. "Are you ready, Ward?"

Mary clutched at Livery's arm and he tried without success to push her away gently. Milt took her by the hand and moved her behind the counter. "John, no, don't," she pleaded.

"You can't hide behind her skirts anymore, Ward," Royce said, and his eyes narrowed to evil slits.

"That'll be the day I hide from the likes of you."

"Oh, so now you're brave all of a sudden."

Mary broke from Milt's grasp and ran to Livery and clutched desperately at his arm again. "Please, John, don't even talk to him. Just walk away."

Royce glanced at the clock on the wall. "You've got one hour, Ward." Mary's eyes were filled with panic as Livery moved her gently to one side. "Be out in the street in one hour," Royce said, "or I'll come in and get you." Then he turned and strode casually out of the store, leaving the door open behind him.

The room fell silent, but suddenly filled with tension. Milt heaved a huge sigh as Mary grasped Livery's arm again. "Now do you see why I'm so scared, so frantic with worry? You can't do this, John."

He took her by the shoulders and held her at arm's length. "I have to." Then he turned and started toward his room.

Mary choked back a sob. "No, John! No! No! Oh, God, John, please don't!" But Livery ignored her pleading and went into his room and closed the door. Mary turned and raced out of the store.

"Wait!" Milt called, as she ran out onto the board sidewalk. "Mary, wait!" he said again, following her outside. "There's something I have to tell you!" But she was already in the street, running toward Sheriff Travis Dutton's office. Milt went back inside, headed for Livery's room, and charged in without knocking. He was rummaging through his saddlebag.

"John, John. This is wrong. I was wrong." Livery pulled his gun belt out of the saddlebag and strapped it on, and Milt felt weak, sick with anxiety and fear, ashamed of the part he had played in this deadly drama that was racing now toward its horrible climax. "Please, John, give it up."

"Sorry, Milt. It's all spilled milk. We can't put it back in the bottle now."

Milt took a deep breath and squared his shoulders. "Don't be too sure," he said while Livery checked the load in his six-shooter. Then he turned, and with long, deliberate strides walked out of the room and out the front door of the general store.

Mary pushed open the door of the sheriff's office and swept in. Travis Dutton was standing at his desk putting assorted books and papers into a small carpetbag. He looked up, his eyes wide with surprise. "Mary! What in blazes is going on?"

"You've got to stop it!" she exclaimed as she gasped for breath.

"Here, now," Travis said, "what's all this?" He came around the desk and took her hands in his. "You look like the devil himself is after you."

"Travis, you've got to stop it," Mary said again.

"Whatever needs stoppin' in this town is goin' to have to be stopped without me. I've had enough of bein' sheriff. I'm leavin' Purgatory. As a matter of fact, I was plannin' on askin' you to come with me."

"No, Travis, you can't leave now. You've got to stop it."

"I have to stop what?"

"There's going to be a gunfight. Please, Travis, you've got to stop it from happening."

"Take it easy," he said gently. "What gunfight are you talking about here?"

"There's going to be a gunfight between John . . . and that terrible man."

"John? Oh, you mean Ward, or Livery, or whatever his name is?"

"Yes," Mary said breathlessly, "and that . . . that gunfighter."

The sheriff's eyes lit up. "Are you talking about the one they call Royce?"

"Yes, and John could get . . ." She couldn't bring herself to say it.

Travis shrugged. "If they want to kill themselves it's no concern of mine."

"But you're still the sheriff. You've got to do something!" Mary was practically screaming.

Travis stood thinking for a moment, and then his mouth twisted into a thin smile. "Maybe I will at that," he said. "I might just stick around and see who's still standin' when the gunplay's all over. I hear that Royce character is mighty fast."

"You don't care if John gets killed . . . ? It'll be like murder."

"I told you Ward was trouble, Mary. I knew it the day he came to town all shot up. Drifters like him usually get what's comin' to 'em. There's no call for me to interfere in their fight."

"You men are all alike," Mary said, her voice rising in anger. "Stand up for your precious manhood—even if it means killing each other!"

Travis took her by her shoulders. "Ward's no kind of man for you, Mary. Can't you see that? Forget about him. You and me could . . ."

"You're disgusting!" Mary shrieked and broke from the sheriff's grasp and raced out the door and into the street. In a few minutes, breathless and feeling the perspiration dampening her hair, she was at the church. She breathed a short prayer of thanks to find the door unlocked and let herself in and went to a front pew and knelt down. An instant later, she heard the soft tread of footsteps behind her and turned to see her father approaching.

"Mary," Milt said, his voice filled with relief. "Thank God you're here. I've been looking all over for you." He went to her and put a gentle hand to her cheek.

Mary's heart froze. "Is he . . . ?" She stepped back and

stared at her father, afraid to ask the question that filled her breast with fear and nearly cut off her breathing. "He's not . . . ?"

"He's okay—for now. But he's still determined to fight Royce."

"Oh, Dad, you've got to stop him—please—somehow."

Milt looked suddenly awkward, embarrassed. "Mary, I . . . I've done all I can." His shoulders sagged and he studied his fingers. His voice was soft in the quiet nave. "He came to me yesterday after church and explained why he couldn't back down from Royce."

"And you didn't talk him out of it?"

Milt's eyes were sad. "Royce killed his brother, Mary."

"I know that," she argued, "but is that reason enough . . . ?"

"That's not all," Milt interrupted. "John's a . . . he's a gunfighter."

Mary was devastated. "Oh, my God!"

Milt took one of her hands in his. "He was the black sheep of the family—broke his father's heart. Now he feels that avenging his brother's killing is the only way he can make it up."

Mary couldn't believe her father's tone of voice. "You mean you condone this madness?"

"I mean I understand it," he said, and paused for a deep breath. "And there's something else." Mary wasn't sure she wanted to hear any more. "When John was shot," Milt continued, "he . . . well, he lost his speed with his gun hand. And he . . . well, he came to me for help . . ."

"No!" Mary screamed. "You didn't! Don't tell me that! How could you?"

Milt hung his head, covered his face with his hands. "I was wrong. I know that now."

"Maybe it's still not too late," Mary said and started for the door. She paused and Milt looked up. "Will you come with me," she asked, "please?"

Milt nodded. "You go ahead. I'll be right behind you."

Royce glanced quickly around his room, checking to make sure he hadn't left anything behind except for the empty whiskey bottle on the stand beside the bed. He wouldn't be coming back here. Once he took care of Ward he was heading out of town. The faint odor of rose perfume still lingered in the room, and as he went to the door he smiled at the recollection of Priscilla's visit.

Downstairs, the saloon already had its share of Monday morning rummies trying to ease the pain of their weekend debauchery. Royce went to the bar and ordered a whiskey. The bartender gave him a bottle and glass and Royce slapped down some coins. He took the watch out of his shirt pocket and checked the time, then downed his drink. As he started across the room toward the swinging doors, a voice called out.

"Royce!" It was Priscilla. He turned to see her standing in the doorway of her office at the end of the bar. "You're supposed to be gone," she said angrily as she strode in his direction.

Royce shrugged, then smiled, faintly amused at her anger. "That's what happens when you break the golden rule," he said, actually enjoying the hatred in Priscilla's glare. "In your business *and* mine, you *never* render a . . . let's call it a service . . . until *after* you've been paid. I would've thought you'd know better." Then he touched the brim of his hat and headed for the door.

Outside on the board sidewalk he checked his watch again. He had ten minutes to wait. He chuckled to himself at the thought of how Ward was probably sweating and worrying. He leaned against a post by the steps and watched with amused interest as Mary Wells scurried along the sidewalk on the opposite side of the street, heading toward the general store. She was followed by her father, his frock coat flapping from the motion of his long, rapid strides.

Royce took out his six-shooter and spun the cylinder to make sure it was fully loaded, even though he knew that it would only take one shot to finish the job that Archer had paid him to do.

Then he went down the steps and out into the street.

Chapter Sixteen

Ward walked from his room into the main part of the general store and looked at the clock on the wall. It was three minutes before the hour. He felt tense, on edge. But that was good—he needed that jolt of excitement and anticipation to sharpen his reflexes and provide whatever little advantage it might give him. As he finished tying down his holster, the front door flew open and Mary and her father burst into the room. Milt crossed quickly to Ward and grasped him firmly by the arm.

"John, I can't let you . . ."

"We've been all over this, Milt."

Mary clutched at his other arm. "Please, just listen to him . . ."

The harsh sound of Royce's voice from outside cut her plea short. "Ward," he roared, "it's time!"

"Oh, no," Mary said, and squeezed her eyes shut.

"Don't go out there, John," Milt urged. "You don't have to prove anything. We both know that."

Ward shrugged free of their restraining fingers and

moved to where he could see out through the large display window. Royce stood spread legged in the middle of the street, hands on his hips and a cruel, malevolent sneer on his face. "You hear me, Ward?" he bellowed again. "It's time. You can't hide now."

Ward turned at the touch of Milt's hand on his shoulder. "I'm not going to let you do this," the older man said quietly.

"Please, Milt," Ward answered, and gently shrugged off his hand.

"I'm asking you one last time," Milt persisted.

Ward shook his head and started toward the door. Milt moved quickly to block him and stood in the open doorway.

"You're in my way," Ward said, his voice soft but menacing.

Milt pulled back his frock coat to reveal a holstered .45 strapped to his waist and tied down to his thigh.

Mary sucked in a huge breath. "Oh, dear Lord, not you too!"

Milt's hand hovered over his gun. "There's no other way, Mary. If I let him go out there you'll never forgive me. I'll never forgive myself." He backed a step deeper into the opening of the doorway.

Ward looked past Milt out into the street. A small crowd was starting to gather. Matt Hennessey came out of his restaurant wiping his hands on his apron, curiosity written plainly on his plump, ruddy face. Across the street, Travis Dutton, chewing casually on a match, leaned against the hitch rail in front of his office. Priscilla Scanlon, in an elegant dress and matching handbag, emerged through the swinging doors of the saloon and walked regally out into the street and took up a position on the edge of the crowd.

Milt motioned for Mary to back away, toward the safety of the counter. "John," he said firmly, "I made one mistake, and I'm not going to make another. I'll stop you, even if I have to . . ."

"You're welcome to try," Ward said and advanced a step toward the door. "But please, Milt, don't do anything foolish."

Milt started to draw his Colt, but Ward's gun was in his hand and cocked by the time the older man's weapon was barely out of its holster. Mary's scream was drowned by the explosion of a single shot, and the .45 went flying out of Milt's fist.

"Sorry I had to do that," Ward said. He holstered his gun and stepped quickly around the grimacing store-keeper and out onto the board sidewalk. The crowd was larger now, lining both sides of the dusty street where Royce stood in an exaggerated slouch that made him appear almost bored. When he saw Ward he grinned sarcastically. "I'm glad to see you're still alive, Ward. I heard a shot. I thought maybe you got so scared you killed yourself."

A movement at the edge of the crowd caught Ward's eye. He looked up in time to see Clay Archer break from behind the sheriff's office and walk quickly to where Travis Dutton was standing. Ward made a quick vow to attend to Archer later—if there was a later. He stepped off the sidewalk and took a few paces into the street.

Royce started in his direction, then stopped and squared his shoulders. His face was grim now, and his eyes were cold and mean. "You picked a good town to die in, Ward—Purgatory, one step from hell." Then he cackled obscenely.

"We'll see who dies," Ward said as the crowd pressed tighter to either side of the street to positions that offered greater safety. Hennessey wiped at his face with his apron and Travis Dutton took out his six-shooter, checked it for load, then re-holstered it. Priscilla Scanlon looked on with her usual composure, but Ward thought he detected a hint of fear in her emerald eyes. The sound of footsteps on the board sidewalk behind him caused him to turn. Mary and her father, a bloodstained rag wrapped around his hand, walked quickly from the general store. Tears glistened in Mary's eyes and she moved to the edge of the sidewalk.

"Don't do this, John," she pleaded, her voice husky and threatening to crack. "Think of your brother."

"He's the one I'm doing it for," Ward said gruffly.

"Is he really, John? Is this what he would want you to do? Is this what he would do?"

Ward didn't answer. He was suddenly filled with a small, nagging doubt, and he stared intently into her pleading eyes.

"Don't throw away this chance for a new life," Mary said, fighting to hold back a sob, "please . . . for my sake."

Ward wanted to turn away from her, but he couldn't. Her eyes were misty, but she was resolute and her gaze held his. Her look tore at him, and he could feel the pain behind her pleading. "If not for me," Mary went on, "then do it for her." She pointed to where Priscilla Scanlon stood in the crowd. Now tears began to flow more freely down Mary's cheeks. "I love you, John," she said, fighting to control her sobbing, "but I'd rather that she have you, than . . ." She couldn't go on.

For the moment Ward forgot that there was a determined killer waiting for him in the middle of the street. All he could think about was his brother—and Mary, and about how she would rather that he go to Priscilla Scanlon than fight Royce. He had never known anyone to love him that much before.

"You know she's right, John," Milt added softly. "You're throwing away a marvelous chance at a new life—the kind of life you should have had."

Ward's mind was filled with a fleeting image of his

father handing him and his brother each brand new concho-decorated holsters packed with gleaming Colt .45s. "These have the power for good or evil, boys. Always make the right choice." The image vanished, and Ward turned back toward the leering man in the street. Slowly he raised his hands away from his body. "I'm not going to fight you, Royce," he said firmly. "It's over."

Royce scowled, and his eyes narrowed to slits of burning hatred, filled with evil.

Slowly Ward undid his holster tie-down and, with his left hand, unbuckled his gun belt and let it slide to the ground. From behind him he heard Mary whisper, "Oh, thank God."

Royce crouched, his hand over his gun, suspicion and disbelief clouding his face. "That's not going to save you, Ward. I told you, gun or no gun . . ."

"You shoot now and it's murder," Ward replied.

"Says who?" Royce growled. "You had your chance. It's a fair fight."

Hennessey wiped at his face again and yelled to Travis Dutton, who was still leaning against the hitch rail. "Ain't you goin' to stop it, Sheriff?"

"It's none of my affair."

"But Ward's unarmed!" Hennessey insisted.

"That's his problem," Dutton answered, and the lines around his eyes crinkled as his mouth twisted into a cynical smile. "He should've thought of that before he dropped his gun belt."

A murmur arose from the crowd and there were a few gasps as Royce calmly and deliberately drew his six-shooter and took careful aim at Ward. The sound of a sudden shot brought other gasps and more than one scream. Royce shuddered, then winced and hunched his shoulders as though in pain. Staggering slightly, he turned toward the crowd, his eyes searching. His gaze came to rest on Priscilla Scanlon. In one hand she was holding her small bag, open now, while in the other hand she clutched a smoking double-barreled derringer. It was pointed at Royce. She fired again, and he flinched from the impact of the second small-caliber bullet. Smiling arrogantly, he raised his weapon in Priscilla's direction.

"No, Royce, don't!" Ward yelled, and dropped to his knees and jerked his six-shooter out of its holster. Royce ignored the shout, but before he could fire at Pricilla, Ward squeezed the trigger. The sound of the shot was loud in the street compared to the report of the derringer. The .45 caliber slug spun Royce around and, with surprise and disbelief etched in his evil face, he stood staring at Ward. He wavered for a moment, then tried to raise his gun. Ward fired again, and this time the lead tore into Royce's chest, knocking him backward and slamming him to the street. He twitched once, then lay still.

Ward breathed a deep sigh and let his gun hang limply in his hand, trying to relax his tense muscles. He heard a sob and turned. Mary and her father seemed frozen on the spot. Tears glistened on her cheeks and her eyes were glued on Ward.

"I . . . I'm sorry," she whispered, "so sorry. I . . . I almost got you killed."

She shuddered and Milt put an arm around her shoulders. "That doesn't mean you were wrong," he said gently.

Ward picked up his gun belt, holstered his six-shooter, and slung it over his shoulder. Now that the fight was over he felt empty inside. Not only had he foolishly risked his own life, but he had nearly been the cause of Priscilla Scanlon getting killed. "I'm the one who was wrong," he admonished himself bitterly, loud enough for Mary to hear, "trying to be something I'm not."

Down the street most of the crowd had already drifted away. Ward watched as the sheriff went to Priscilla and took the derringer out of her hand while Hennessey looked on. Archer was nowhere to be seen.

"Go to her, John," Mary said.

He turned and looked deep into her eyes.

She pointed down the street. "Go to her. I could never be the kind of woman she is, never do what she did for you." Then she buried her face in her hands, and with her shoulders quaking, ran back into the store.

"You weren't wrong, John," Milt said. "No matter what you think, you tried to do the right thing. And you're a better man for it. From what you've told me, it's the kind of thing your brother would have done. You can take satisfaction in that." He started for the store, then stopped and looked back. "And I know you did it for Mary. You love her, John. Whether or not you admit it, you love her." Then he went inside.

Ward thought about the preacher's words, and then he walked slowly to where Travis Dutton was kneeling over Royce's body. Priscilla and Hennessey looked on while he went through the dead man's pockets.

She acknowledged Ward with a nod and started to leave.

"Wait," he said, and stopped her with a hand on her arm. "I just wanted to thank you for what you did for me."

Priscilla stared at him coolly. "What did I do for you?"

"Shooting Royce—you saved my life."

"I shot Royce because he lied to me, broke his promise. Nobody breaks his word to me and gets away with it."

"But you could have been killed."

"Would you have cared?"

The question startled Ward. "Yes," he said, after a long pause, "yes, I would have cared very much."

Priscilla's lip trembled as she tried to smile. "Then

I'm glad 1 shot him," she said, her green eyes suddenly misty, and she started again for the saloon.

He watched her for a moment and pondered the events of the last few minutes. His brother's killer lay dead, and it was now apparent that there were two women in love with him. Maybe Milt Wells was right, after all; maybe he was at the crossroads of a new life.

Then he turned his attention to Hennessey and Dutton, who was completing his search of Royce's body. "What a shame," the Irishman said wistfully, almost as if he was talking to himself.

"You can't be serious," Ward exclaimed.

"He's the only customer I ever had who liked me stew," Hennessey replied, and chuckled at his own joke.

Dutton looked up and glared. "I warned you about lettin' that gun get you into trouble, Ward," he said, getting to his feet. "Hand it over." Dutton drew his six-shooter and aimed it at Ward's chest. "You're under arrest for murder."

"You're crazy," Ward protested. "You saw what happened."

"I saw a man tryin' to protect himself from a woman who was about to kill him. Let me have that gun."

"She had a two-shot derringer. And she had already fired both shots. The gun was empty and Royce was still standing."

Out of the corner of his eye, Ward saw Hennessey back away slowly and retreat toward his restaurant. "You know Royce was a hired gun," Ward protested. "And you know Archer sent him to kill me. He's the one you want."

"This's got nothin' to do with Archer."

Ward exploded. "He had my brother killed! He tried to kill me! And you know he's behind the rustling at Kelso's ranch."

"I know me and Archer had a sweet setup until your nosey brother got in the way—and now you." Travis advanced a couple of steps. "Hand over the gun."

Ward turned and started away. "I'm going for the marshal."

"You're not goin' anywhere," the sheriff said, "except back to prison to hang . . . if you live long enough, that is." Dutton cocked the hammer on his six-shooter. Ward paused at the sound. "I'd like nothin' better," Dutton said, "than to shoot you right now for tryin' to escape. And you know why." He reached for Ward's revolver.

"Hold it right there, Sheriff." Ward turned to see Hennessey holding his shotgun on Dutton. "I was sayin' to John just the other day that the town might be needin' a new sheriff one of these days. Now I'm sure of it."

Dutton's face went pale and his brow wrinkled over eyes that were suddenly filled with panic.

Ward eased his six-shooter out of the holster slung over his shoulder. "Get his gun, Matt," he said, and pointed his Colt at the sheriff.

Hennessey lowered his shotgun and reached for the sheriff's weapon. Dutton knocked his hand away, slipped quickly behind him, and wrapped an arm around the startled Irishman's neck. He pressed the muzzle of his .45 to Hennessey's head. "Put that gun down, Ward." Dutton backed toward the horses tied at the nearest hitch rail, dragging his gasping, stumbling captive with him, and Hennessey's shotgun dropped to the dusty street.

"Empty your iron, or your friend here gets plugged," Dutton growled. "Do it now!"

Ward opened the cylinder of his .45 and flushed the shells out onto the ground.

"Now toss it over here," Dutton demanded, and Ward threw his gun at the sheriff's feet.

Without warning, Dutton hit Hennessey with a blow to the back of the head from his six-shooter that dropped him to his knees. Then he mounted the nearest horse and, spurring the animal viciously, raced toward the road leading out of town.

"Are you all right?" Ward said as he helped Hennessey to his feet, wobbly but able to stand.

"Aye, thank God for a hard Irish skull," Hennessey said, rubbing the back of his head.

Ward retrieved his Colt and started to reload. "Tell

Milt Wells what happened here. Have him send for the marshal. I'm going after Travis."

"What's this now?" Hennessey was wide-eyed. "The last I recall you weren't too interested in getting involved in the sheriff's affairs. Now you're all hot to track him down. How come the change of heart?"

"Sometimes things happen to change a man," Ward said as he strapped on his gun belt. Then he put a hand on Matt's shoulder. "Are you sure you're all right?"

Hennessey nodded and Ward started in the direction of the livery stable. "Hold on," Hennessey called out, holding the hitch rail for support, "and give me a minute to clear me head, and I'll go with you."

"There's no time," Ward replied over his shoulder. "Just tell Milt I'll be back before dark . . . or not at all. And tell Mary . . . Never mind."

Ward made straight for the line camp on the Kelso ranch. He had to start looking somewhere, and he was playing a hunch that since Archer and Dutton were both out of town at the same time there was a good chance that they could be planning to meet at the shack. With their partnership in the rustling scheme exposed, and now with Royce dead, there was no telling what the sheriff and the Kelso foreman might be cooking up to try to keep Ward from going to the U.S. marshal.

About fifty yards from the shack, he reined up in a

stand of Palo Verde trees where he could observe the dilapidated building without being seen. There was only a single horse tied up at the hitch rail, and it wasn't the one Dutton had commandeered in town. *So much for my bright ideas,* Ward said to himself, frustrated at not finding two horses at the line camp. Now uncertain as to who the owner of the lone horse might be, he worked his way stealthily to the rear of the shack, secured his horse out of sight, and quietly made his way up to a grimy window. He took his hat off and peeked through the cracked glass. Archer was at a table stuffing wads of bills into a saddlebag. *Well, at least I was half right,* Ward told himself. Archer stopped what he was doing, looked up, and cocked his head to one side, listening. Somewhere a horse nickered; Ward heard it too.

Suddenly the door burst open and Dutton strode in, a thin, accusing sneer on his face. "Are you goin' somewhere partner?"

Archer wheeled, eyes bulging. "Oh, it's you. I wondered where you were."

"I stopped out at the Kelso place first, then figgered you might be hidin' out here. Looks like you're packin' up."

"Yeah, with Ward on the loose out there somewhere this cattle scheme's all washed up. I'm clearin' out."

Dutton walked warily around the table, his eyes

never leaving Archer's face. "You weren't thinkin' of leavin' with my share of the money, now were you?"

"Would I do that? What's the matter—don't you trust me?"

"Sure I do," Dutton said, letting his hand rest on the butt of his six-shooter "especially after you tried to kill me."

"Aw," Archer replied, with a feeble grin, "that was all for show—just to keep Ward from thinkin' we was in cahoots."

Ward left his position at the window and slipped around to the front of the shack, quietly approached the open door, and, out of the line of sight of the two men inside, stood watching. "Here," Archer said, motioning to Dutton, "let me give you what you got comin'," and he reached into the saddlebag on the table. When he withdrew his hand it was filled with his Colt .45 and he swung it toward the sheriff. But he was too slow. Dutton drew his gun and fired before Archer could get off a shot. The blast knocked him back over the table, already dead, and with blood soaking the front of his shirt.

"Drop it, Dutton!" Ward barked from the doorway. The sheriff whirled and fired, but his shot went wild, splintering the door frame inches above Ward's head. Ward's gun spoke and the Colt went flying out of the sheriff's hand.

Dutton groaned in agony, holding his bloody fingers. "I told Archer he should've killed you a long time ago," he hissed through clenched teeth.

"How do you know he didn't?" Ward said with a humorless chuckle. "Maybe I'm a triplet." He went to the saddlebag and looked inside. There were several bundles of bills of various denominations wrapped in rubber bands.

"Listen, Ward," Dutton said while he struggled to wrap his bandanna around his wounded hand, "there's a lot of money there. Why don't we split it up and . . . you know, you go your way . . ."

"This is Kelso ranch money," Ward said. He scooped the remaining bills off the table and put them in the saddlebag, closed it up, and threw it over his shoulder. "It's going where it belongs." Then, with his six-shooter, he motioned Dutton toward the open door. "And so are you."

Chapter Seventeen

Matt Hennessey tied a pair of old shoes to the back of the buggy that stood just a few feet from the front steps of the church. Then he straightened up the hand-lettered *Just Married* sign he had made and stood back and smiled at his handiwork.

Just then the bell in the steeple began to ring and the front door flew open. A smiling crowd poured out and lined both sides of the steps and turned expectantly to face the open door. A cheer went up from the group when Livery appeared and stepped out onto the church landing. He was dressed in a frock coat and string tie. He smiled and waved at the crowd, shook a few hands, then turned to gaze at the woman at his side. She was dressed all in white, from the lacy veil that hung from her tiny bonnet to the dainty slippers that peeked out from under the billowing skirt of her dress.

A few members of the smiling crowd threw handfuls of rice as the couple dodged their way down the steps.

Milt, dressed in his preacher's finery, came out of the church and stood beaming. Then he followed the newly-weds as they dashed to where Hennessey stood at the waiting buggy. "Congratulations, you two," Matt said and embraced them both while Milt looked on approvingly.

The groom turned to his bride, lifted her veil, and kissed her gently on the lips. "Happy wedding day, Mrs. Ward."

Mary smiled up at him. "It's Mrs. Livery, remember? You have a new name and a new life. There is no more Justin Ward."

"You're right, Mary," he said in a soft voice. "It's as though the Ward brothers are gone now. I like to think they both died good men." As he stood momentarily lost in thought, he caught sight of Priscilla Scanlon just leaving the church. She paused for a moment and glanced in his direction, then with a sad smile and a nod she moved quickly through the crowd and was lost in the throng of buggies and wagons that were tied at the side of the building.

"By the way," Hennessey said exuberantly, rubbing his hands together eagerly, "the whole weddin' party's invited over to me restaurant for all the stew you can eat—on the house."

"I ought to run you in, Hennessey," Livery said grinning, and pulled back his frock coat to reveal a sheriff's star pinned to his vest. "There's got to be a law against selling food that tastes that awful."

The whole crowd broke into hearty laughter—even Hennessey.